TAILING PHILIP MARLOWE

Three tours of Los Angeles based
on the work of Raymond Chandler

Brian and Bonnie Olson

Brittany —
Best wishes.

Bonnie Olson

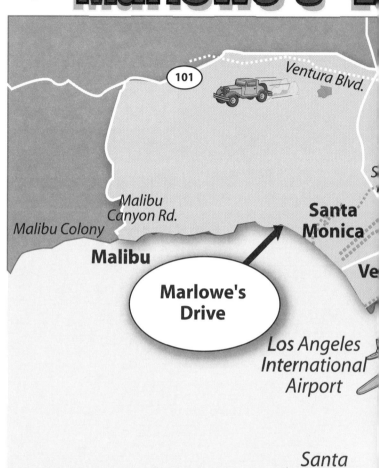

Marlowe's L

101

Ventura Blvd.

Malibu Canyon Rd.

Malibu Colony

Malibu

Santa Monica

Marlowe's Drive

Ve

Los Angeles International Airport

Santa Monica Bay

Pacific Ocean

Published in the United States by Burlwrite LLC, St. Paul, Minnesota.

Olson, Brian and Bonnie
Tailing Philip Marlowe.
Title

Book and jacket design by Meleck Davis
Page design by Laurie Schlueter-Hynes

ISBN 0-9729239-0-X (pbk.)

Manufactured in the United States of America

Tailing Philip Marlowe Contents

Foreword

The little sidewalk car came trundling along the wide concrete walk. I got on it and rode to the end of the line and got off and sat on a bench where it was quiet and cold and there was a big brown heap of kelp almost at my feet. Out to sea they had turned the lights on in the gambling boats. I got back on the sidewalk car the next time it came and rode back to almost to where I had left the hotel. If anybody was tailing me, he was doing it without moving. I didn't think there was.

(Farewell, My Lovely)

Despite his modest production, or perhaps because of the time he took to craft his work, Raymond Chandler stands as a premier writer of the modern detective genre. The character he created, that of the hard-boiled, cynical private eye, remains the mold from which many detectives in modern fiction have sprung. In addition to this, Chandler brought a discerning mind and a talent for describing his characters and surroundings, especially through metaphor, that is unsurpassed.

Although born in Chicago, Illinois, Chandler was raised in England and spent some of his youth traveling in Europe, part of the "rounding out" of British youth. Following service in World War I, he settled in California. In the American west, particularly in Los Angeles, the juxtaposition of his continental upbringing versus this new culture, with its free-wheeling mores, liberated architecture and vulgar manners, must have been a wellspring of material and at the same time a catalyst for his work. With this in mind, it would appear to be no accident that many of the buildings and locations chosen for his novels are, or were during his time, the most vibrant examples of their type existing in the city.

During these three tours Chandler fans will be viewing some of the outstanding examples of buildings mentioned in his work; many have been preserved or restored and retain the spirit of that age. Some, unfortunately, no longer exist; where this has happened, we have attempted to find examples that most closely match the structures he described. Missing, too, are the open areas of Chandler's city (Into the 1940s one could still ride a horse on bridle paths north from the Beverly Hills Hotel to the hills overlooking the city). These spaces have disappeared, but there still remain the streets and highways used for the long reflective drives that Raymond Chandler and his fictional character, Philip Marlowe, took through and around the city. On the final tour, you will see the City in which he lived and about which he wrote from the heights of the Santa Monica range and from the ocean shore at Malibu, and perhaps also from a new perspective regarding his work.

Bonnie and Brian Olson
St. Paul, Minnesota
June 2003

Using this Guide

Tailing Philip Marlowe is designed as a three-day driving and walking tour of Los Angeles and its environs. It is organized around three sections of the metropolitan area that served as focus points for Chandler's work. A map is at the start of each tour and driving and walking instructions are included in the text. A comprehensive map of the Los Angeles area is desirable; we used the Rand McNally Los Angeles/Hollywood City Map for our work, and found it most helpful.

We have designated some of the stops as **Marlowe Must-Sees.** These are so designated because they are of particular importance in Chandler's works and also because they have architectural or historical importance regarding the Los Angeles landscape of the Thirties. Those not having time for the three-day tour may desire to select a shorter route using these stops (See page 5). Other stops have been designated **Marlowe Might-Have-Beens** because they are particularly significant for that time, or because there is a probability that they played a role in influencing Chandler in his writing.

Listings
All headings in this book are the actual names or addresses of buildings or places. These are followed by the Raymond Chandler/Philip Marlowe name and/or description and the title of the work in which it is found.

A One-Day Marlowe Tour

Those not having the time or not desiring to spend three straight days following Marlowe's trail may wish to consider visiting some or all of the following sites. They represent the locations of the Marlowe Must-Sees and one Marlowe Might-Have-Been.

Wiltern Theater, 3790 Wilshire Boulevard

Bullock's Wilshire, 3050 Wilshire Boulevard

Los Angeles City Hall, 200 N. Spring Street

The Bradbury Building, 304 South Broadway

Oviatt Building, 617 Olive Street

Union Station, 800 North Alameda Avenue

Cahuenga Building, 6381-6385 Hollywood Boulevard

Doheny Mansion (Greystone), 905 Loma Vista Avenue

Beverly Hills Hotel, 9641 Sunset Boulevard, Beverly Hills

Stairway, The 280 Step, 17572 Pacific Coast Highway at Castellammare

Santa Monica/Venice Beach Walk

Santa Monica Pier

Getting to and around in Los Angeles

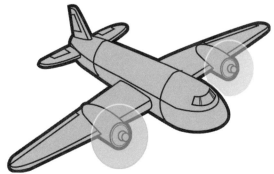

Arriving by Air

Los Angeles International Airport (LAX) serves the region and is about twenty minutes from the Santa Monica/Venice area and thirty minutes from downtown, more if traffic is heavy. Since a vehicle is almost essential for this tour, we recommend renting a car as soon as you arrive. Most of the rental companies have shuttle busses that will take customers to the car rental office. If you can't or don't want to rent a car, see Public Transit and DASH on page 9.

Car Rentals

A variety of car rental offices are within ten minutes of LAX, and there are other offices around the City. Some of the local rental companies provide excellent late model convertibles at reasonable rates. This is an excellent way to take the tour, although in summer months, with the sun more directly overhead, you may have to take some precautions to avoid sunburn.

Arriving by Train

For a truly period experience, plan to arrive by train. Union Station is a well-preserved gem and arriving there will place you into a frame of mind for immediate Marlowe snooping. Although Amtrak has canceled the famous Desert Wind train from Las Vegas, as of this writing it still operates the Sunset Limited, the Coast Starlight and the Southwest Chief. Amtrak has plans to operate a train between Las Vegas and Los Angeles in the near future, but plans for Amtrak itself are uncertain as this work is written.

Traffic

Los Angeles is notorious for its traffic jams; these can happen any time and in anyplace, but in general, try to avoid using the freeways between 7-9 in the morning and 3-6 in the afternoon on weekdays. The surface streets are preferable in any case, first because freeways did not exist in Chandler's time and second because street level driving presents the opportunity to observe a variety of neighborhoods and to gain the "might have been" Marlowe atmosphere.

Public Transit and DASH

Getting around Los Angeles by public transit is possible, but time-consuming. To attempt to use it for some parts of this tour would be very difficult. On the other hand, for touring Marlowe's Downtown and some of Marlowe's Hollywood, transportation such as the LA Transit DASH is a great aid for all but the most stalwart of walkers. DASH busses serve as circulators for various parts of Los Angeles, including Downtown, Hollywood, Chinatown and Studio City. DASH busses generally run every five to ten minutes; fares are 25 cents, which includes a two-hour transfer good for any other DASH route. Service is limited on weekends but does include Downtown. This guide notes the DASH routes you will need. To obtain maps, go to the LADOT website at http://www.ladottransit.com/dash/index.html. For more information, call (213, 310 or 818) 808-2273.

Places to Stay

Los Angeles offers accommodations for practically any budget or taste, whether you select to stay near the airport, the beach, downtown or in Beverly Hills. For a true Marlowe experience, we could route Tailers to one of the remaining downtown hotels where Marlowe did most of his hotel snooping. These are now old dowagers that rent by the week to transient travelers and workers of limited means. Since they represent rough trade, and you probably are not interested in packing a rod, we instead recommend staying in the Santa Monica or Venice area. Perhaps next to the ocean, along the street that Chandler called Speedway in *Farewell My Lovely* and which actually exists. In *Farewell,* Marlowe is staying in Bay City, most likely in one of the hotels built in Venice and Santa Monica during the early part of the 20th century. Some of them remain, retaining their original art deco style, although most have been converted to apartments or condos. For newer and more upscale digs, try the hotels along the beach at Santa Monica, Santa Monica Boulevard, or on the west side of downtown. These locations place one close to the starting points for the tours. They also have the advantage of being relatively close to the Los Angeles airport.

Best Time to Visit

Anytime is a good time to visit Los Angeles. For those not familiar with southern California, consider the following:

- Summer is the busy season, so rates will be highest and availability most limited for hotels. For best selection, arrange to arrive on a Sunday or Monday night.

- Rental car agencies are also at their busiest on Saturdays and Sundays in the summer; the wait will be shortest on weekdays.

- Winter months of December through March, excluding holidays are generally bargain months, with fewer crowds; nights will be cool, but not uncomfortable.

- Rainfall for Los Angeles averages twelve to thirteen inches per year, with about seven to eight inches falling during the winter months of December-February; this is also the most likely season for occasional torrential rains. Rain is a common element in Chandler's work; committed fans may find this the best season to experience his city and hope for drizzly days and nights.

What to Bring

- This guide;
- A map of Los Angeles. We prefer the Rand McNally map of Los Angeles/Hollywood for most complete street information;
- Comfortable shoes for walking;
- A light jacket or sweater and a scarf, cap, or other headgear, especially during the winter months, as it can get chilly when the sun goes down;
- A couple of Raymond Chandler paperbacks.

FOR YOUR HEALTH AND COMFORT, PLEASE READ THE FOLLOWING:

<u>Physical Activity</u> - The first and third day's tours include extensive walking, including stair climbing. Do not perform any stressful physical exercise for which you are not prepared, especially the 280 Steps. Consult your physician if you have any questions about your physical ability to take this tour.

<u>Security</u> - Many of the buildings you will be visiting are public and have security checkpoints. To make your visit more pleasant, we advise against carrying metallic items or other objects that can set off security devices. Cameras and common tourist accouterments are okay.

<u>Safety</u> - In our visits to LA we have felt comfortable in practically all of the locations listed in this book. Panhandlers are common, but not aggressive. As with any urban area, common sense should be used in all situations. Certain areas of the beach may be intimidating after dark and we advise staying near the more well-lit and visited locations when strolling at night along the shore.

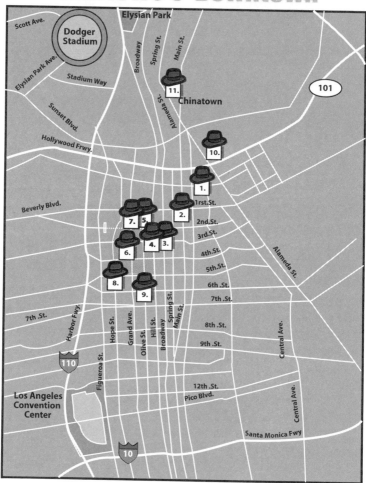

Marlowe's Downtown

1. City Hall
2. Times Building
3. Bradbury Building
4. Grand Central Market
5. Second Street Tunnel
6. Angel's Flight Funicular
7. Bunker Hill
8. Los Angeles Public Library
9. Oviatt Building
10. Union Station
11. Phillipe the Original

Marlowe's Downtown

First Day Tour

This tour takes you by or through most of the downtown locations described by Raymond Chandler. Although Los Angeles is a metropolitan area of 15.8 million people, its downtown footprint is comparable to those of smaller cities, making it surprisingly walkable and amenable to a one-day visit. Our tour starts with City Hall. From there, we will visit various locations mentioned and used by Chandler in *High Window, The King in Yellow, Trouble is My Business* and other works. The tour finishes with a visit to Union Station, mentioned in *Playback,* with optional visits to Central Avenue and the south end, where Florian's Bar stood *(Farewell, My Lovely)* and/or a stop at the La Plata cigar factory.

The Los Angeles Times building

Starting Your Drive

For those staying in Venice or Santa Monica take Pico or Venice Boulevard from Santa Monica to downtown. For a quicker but less authentic trip, find the Santa Monica Freeway and take it east to downtown. Depending upon traffic, you will be downtown in 25-35 minutes. Exit at Grand Avenue, which delivers vehicles to the south side of downtown. There were no freeways when Philip Marlowe drove these streets; taking the secondary route gives one a snapshot of the diversity of Los Angeles as well as a view of some older neighborhoods. Both Pico and Venice intersect with Grand Avenue a few blocks after passing under I-110.

Parking Downtown

For this tour, we recommend using the parking lots just east of downtown along Alameda Avenue. To get there, continue east on Pico Avenue to Central Avenue. This will jog a bit as it goes through the Los Angeles garment district. Pico forms a T intersection at Central, at which point you will see the Coca-Cola bottling plant on the right across the street. *Tailers* may desire to stop and take a look (see page 18). Chandler does not mention the structure in any of his works, and whether he ever drank Coke, even with rum, is unknown, but the building is of the period and is interesting for its over-the-top Streamline Moderne style. After checking it out, continue up Central to Third Street and turn right. Go over one block to Alameda and note several surface parking lots at First and Second Avenues. These are all relatively inexpensive, as opposed to downtown parking; they are also on or near the DASH downtown route. After parking, walk down to Third and Alameda and turn right, towards Central Avenue and downtown. As of this edition, there is a stop for the Blue DASH line on the north side of Third Street between Alameda and Central. Board here and start your tour.

Coca-Cola Bottling (Pico and Central)

If Marlowe had drunk Coke (which he didn't, except perhaps with rum), it would have been bottled here. In 1924, the Los Angeles plant was producing 66,000 gallons per year, employing about 80 workers and using a fleet of 15 vehicles for distribution. By 1930, production had surpassed the 100,000-gallon mark, or 12 million bottles per year. The increase in production led to the need for a larger facility. The current building, constructed in 1936, was designed by Architect Robert Derrah. His design, with distinctly nautical motifs, joined four separate existing structures together in a "Streamline Moderne" style. In fact, the building is patterned after a German ship of the 1890's. The style emerged from an economic need for less

expensive buildings during the depression years. Moderne style made extensive use of stucco, glass block, enamel and other new materials and less of the metalwork, colorful mosaics and zigzag and chevron decoration of Art Deco. During the 1930s building design had shifted to a more horizontal profile. This "wind tunnel" appearance reflected the public's growing fascination with speed and transportation. In 1976, the "Coca-Cola Ship" was declared an historical and cultural monument.

Los Angeles City Hall, 200 N. Spring Street

A MARLOWE MUST-SEE

*I went out, along the corridor and down in the night elevator
to the City Hall lobby. I went out the Spring Street side and
down the long flight of empty steps and the wind blew cold.
I lit a cigarette at the bottom. My car was still out at the
Jeeter place. I lifted a foot to start walking to a taxi half a
block down across the street. A voice spoke sharply from
a parked car. "Come here a minute."*

(Trouble Is My Business)

Ride the DASH about four blocks. The bus will make its way up to First
Street and stop directly in front of City Hall. As you get out, look up and
observe the exuberant American Jazz Age facade of the building.
Completed in 1928, City Hall was until 1957 the only structure in the city
allowed to exceed a 13-story limit. The building consists of a central tower
425 feet in height with wings on the north and south sides which contain
board rooms, city council chambers and offices. Entry is via Main Street,
which should be to your right. Once past security, check out the rotunda in
the center of the building just past the elevator shafts. In the center of the
rotunda is a cast bronze insert of a 16th century Spanish ship, inlaid with
marble. The rotunda is also famous for its acoustics. Returning to the
elevator lobby, note the bronze elevator cabs and doors and the decorations
on walls and ceilings. Do not miss the observation deck on the 29th floor.
Take an express elevator to the 22nd floor, then a local from the 22nd to the
26th floor. A flight of stairs takes you to the observation area where you
will find yourself in the Mayor Tom Bradley Room, from which you can
see the whole city.

Union Station from City Hall Tower

Returning to the lobby, exit via the Spring Street Vestibule, the formal entrance to City Hall. In the vestibule, you will notice large niches at either end. One holds the torch from the 1984 Olympics. The other niche is empty, awaiting an appropriately heroic statue. Walk down the steps Marlowe took in *Trouble is My Business* to Spring Street and on to your next "tail." Get into parked cars at your own risk.

City Hall is open from 8AM to 5PM M-F; the observation deck, which is free, is open from 9 AM-1PM M-F. Call (213) 978-1995 for information on tours.

CORRUPTION IN CITY HALL

In reading Chandler's books one notes, especially in his early works, that the police, legal and political systems are hopelessly corrupt, with everyone from the cop on the beat to judges and elected officials on the take. The police also tend to be ignorant, biased and hostile to Marlowe and to private eyes in general. As with much of his work, there is more than a modicum of reality in this observation. From 1933 to 1938, when Chandler was writing for *Black Mask* and laying out his future novels, Los Angeles was experiencing what would eventually be known as the most corrupt administration in its history. The leader of this was Frank L. Shaw, elected Mayor of Los Angeles in 1933. Among other activities, the Mayor won the *Los Angeles Times* over to his side by arranging for the City to purchase some *Times* property at four times its value. His brother Joe was appointed to the city payroll and oversaw activities in the police and fire departments. Eventually, the county became interested in rumors of corruption and appointed Clifford Clinton to lead a Grand Jury charged with investigating the situation in city hall. A report was subsequently issued linking the administration to gambling and prostitution rackets throughout the city.

The matter might have stopped without much further action but for a car bomb that exploded on January 14, 1937 in the car of Harry Raymond, a private investigator working for opponents of Shaw. Raymond survived the blast and through an eyewitness the perpetrators were identified. A Los Angeles police captain was indicted and convicted for the attack. The publicity surrounding the bombing and the implication that it was directed from higher up led to a recall election in which Shaw was thrown out of office. Judge Bowron, who had appointed the Grand Jury, was elected and commenced a cleanup of the city government. The effects of this cleanup, the increased professionalism of the police force and the onset of World War II are probably all factors in Chandler's gentler handling of the law and Marlowe's interaction with it in his later novels.

The Times Building, Corner of First and Spring

The Tribune office was at Fourth and Spring. Carmady parked
around the corner, went in at the employee's entrance and rode
to the fourth floor in a rickety elevator operated by an old man
with a dead cigar in his mouth and a rolled magazine which he
held six inches from his nose while he ran the elevator.

(Guns at Cyrano's, *The Simple Art of Murder*)

Exiting City Hall on Spring Street, look to the left and you will see the
Times Building across First Street, kitty-corner from the City Hall
block. Cross Spring Street on the north side of the intersection and walk
until you are directly across the street from the northern entrance. The
cornerstone for this building, the fourth occupied by the Times, was laid
on April 10, 1934. It was designed by Gordon B. Kaufmann, an
architect from England who also designed Hoover Dam and Santa Anita
Park. The building was fully occupied in July 1935 and was noted for
its numerous innovations, including being the first newspaper building
to be entirely air-conditioned. For earthquake protection, the building
was constructed in two separate structural units. These are connected
on each floor by metal slip joints, which provide flex. The system has
proven itself during subsequent earthquakes.

Examining the facade, note the stylized eagles on two portals above the
entrance and the captions: "Truth/Liberty Under the Law" and "Equal
Rights/True Industrial Freedom." Kaufmann was a member of the
Board of Supervisors for the WPA, and perhaps the inscription
demonstrates backlash against the union rhetoric of the era; on the other
hand, perhaps it is a pro-union sentiment. Above the portals and
supported by four columns are three heroic nine-foot bas-relief figures,
carved directly into the side of the building. Symbolism was rampant,
idealism still flourished during the thirties despite a world war and a
depression. Within ten years this heroic impulse in architecture would
be abandoned, in part from cynicism that set in following the Second
World War. Raymond Chandler saw darkly through it all, along with
Hammett and Cain.

Walk across First Street to the north entrance. Above the bronze doors are twelve brass plaques representing Los Angeles themes of the Thirties. Above the two figures are two more eagles on pedestals just underneath an enormous clock face. The cornices of the building echo the eagle theme, with stylized wings wrapped around the corners. Look through the bronze front doors into the vestibule (The main entrance to the building is now on Spring Street). This entrance opens into a rotunda called the Globe Lobby, which is appropriately dominated by a large revolving sphere of the Earth. The globe is made of aluminum, 5 ° feet in diameter and set on a bronze pedestal. It rotates once every fifteen minutes. Bas-reliefs, murals and a fabulous mosaic floor in the form of a giant compass complete the lobby. The murals continue the heroic worker theme of the exterior captions depicting a factory with smokestacks, a man in bib overalls, a sailor, a futuristic automobile and add transportation and manufacturing themes.

Beyond these is the marble elevator lobby with silver leaf inlay on the ceiling and bronze inlays on the floor. Displayed on a pedestal in this lobby is a bronze eagle by John Gutzum Borglum (of Mount Rushmore fame). This does not rotate. The eagle stood atop each of the first three Times buildings until 1935, at which time it was brought indoors and placed on its current perch. The museum is not open to the public, but tours are available. Call 1-800-LATIMES in advance for information. Continue your walk around the corner and down Spring Street. Those who have booked a tour will now go into the main entrance of the Times. Those who have not may continue down Spring Street.

Interior view of the Bradbury. Reproduced with permission.

The Bradbury Building,
304 South Broadway

 **A MARLOWE MUST-SEE**

The Belfont Building was eight stories of nothing in particular that had got itself pinched off between a large green and chromium cut rate suit emporium and a three-story and basement garage that made a noise like lion cages at feeding time. The dark narrow lobby was as dirty as a chicken yard. The building directory had a lot of vacant space on it...Opposite the directory a large sign tilted against the fake marble wall said: Space for Renting Suitable for Cigar Stand. Apply Room 316.

There were two open grill elevators but only one seemed to be running and that not busy. An old man sat inside it slack-jawed and watery-eyed on a piece of folded burlap on top of a wooden stool. He looked as if he had been sitting there since the Civil War and had come out of that badly.

(The High Window)

Proceed down Spring Street to Third Street, and take a right. Walk one block to Broadway. As one approaches Broadway, the Bradbury Building is on the left hand side, across the street on the corner of Third Street and Broadway. It is described by Marlowe as the Belfont Building in High Window in not the most flattering terms; perhaps it was in poor condition during the thirties. An unassuming Italian Renaissance exterior on the outside, the building's interior is a marvel of ironwork and terra cotta. You may enter the building from entrances on Broadway or on Third Street.

Walking into the lobby, notice how the daylight from the skylight floods the warm caramel-colored interior, punctuated by intricate grillwork on the elevator cages and the railings on each floor. The atrium-style building is the design of George Wyman, who was hired by Lewis Bradbury, a mining millionaire. The building was commissioned by Bradbury in 1892 and completed in 1893. Inspiration for the building came from an 1880s science fiction novel, *"Looking Backward,"* by Edward Bellamy. (The book was one of the three best-sellers of the second half of the nineteenth century. The mock preface of the book is dated December, 26, 2000. Francis Bellamy, the brother of Edward, was the composer of the Pledge of Allegiance.) George Wyman was inspired by a description in the book of future commercial buildings as vast atrium structures with domes letting in light from above and followed this impulse in his design. The wrought iron grillwork was manufactured in France and displayed at the Chicago World's Fair before being installed in the building. Ill and aging, the builder, Lewis Bradbury, died a few months prior to completion of the structure and never saw his monument in its final form.

Don't miss the freestanding mail drops, which ascend five stories with minimal support. The building has been used as a set for several movies, including *Blade Runner* and *Chinatown*. The 1969 movie *Marlowe* used the building for some of the interior scenes.

When you have completed your visit, proceed out the Broadway Avenue exit and across the street to the Central Market, the Second Street tunnel and Angel's Flight.

The Bradbury Building, Broadway and Third Street

Grand Central Market, Broadway and Third Streets

If you are ready for a snack or meal, exit the Bradbury building on Broadway, cross the street to enter the Grand Central market. The market has been in existence since 1917 and was a fixture when Marlowe walked the streets. Always bustling, it's a great place to purchase some food or drink; you will find lawyers and businessmen, tourists and locals all seeking out their favorite cuisine. Inside the doors almost any kind of food is available: Tacos and enchiladas, teriyaki, sushi and Chinese food, hot dogs, espresso or ice cream. Strolling musicians add to the flavor. Walking the sawdust floors you can watch the vendors cut and wrap pork hocks, tripe, fish, tongue, and squid, and more. Others are selling frijoles, pescado, fritos, tortillas chilies, spices, fruits and vegetables. The activities all intermingle into an international potpourri of aromas, sights and sound. After stopping to browse, eat or observe, walk straight through the market to Hill Street. Here the west facade of the market faces California Plaza. Across the street is Angel's Flight. From here, *Tailers* may check out the Second Street tunnel or proceed directly to Angel's Flight.

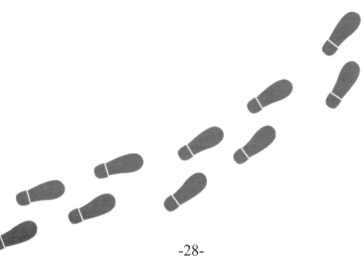

Second Street Tunnel

*Mars flicked the Luger out again and pointed it at my chest.
"Open the door." The knob rattled and a voice called out. I
didn't move. The muzzle of the Luger looked like the mouth of
the Second Street tunnel, but I didn't move. Not being bullet
proof is an idea I had had to get used to.*

(The Big Sleep)

Exit the market on Hill street. To see the tunnel, walk one block north
(or right), to Second Street and turn left. In front of you and across
Hill Street is the tunnel. This tunnel, and the others that bore under
Bunker Hill, were constructed as solutions to the problem of going
around or over Bunker Hill on the way to the western reaches of the
City. In the days of gravel streets, running roads straight up the hill
left something to be desired, given the tendency of the adobe soil to
form ruts when rained upon, not to mention the dust generated when
they were dry. Angel's Flight (next stop) provided a pedestrian access
solution for most of the folks living on top of the hill. For traffic, the
City concluded that three tunnels should be constructed to provide
access to downtown from the west. In 1901, a tunnel was blasted into
the hill at Third Street. Planning for the Second Street tunnel started
in 1916 and actual construction began in 1922. The specifications
called for a bore width of fifty feet clear and a length of 1502.45 feet
from portal to portal. The tunnel was to be wide enough to provide
for a double-track street railway with additional room for automobile
lanes. It was also to be tile lined and suitably lighted. After some
delays, including cave-ins of soft earth, which threatened to collapse
the timbering of the drifts, difficulty in obtaining bricks of satisfactory
quality for the arches and contractor issues, the project was completed
in 1925. During construction, provisions had to be made for air shafts
to provide ventilation for motor vehicles, which had increased
markedly in number from the time the first plans were drawn up. The
Los Angeles Times noted that completion of the tunnel gave access to
people from as far away as Sunset Boulevard and "relieved
congestion" in the downtown district.

Return down Hill Street. Across from the Central Market is Angel's
Flight.

Looking up Angel's Flight from Hill Street

Angel's Flight Funicular Railway, Third and Hill Streets

...I parked at the end of the street, where the funicular railway comes struggling up the yellow clay bank from Hill Street, and walked along Court Street to the Florence Apartments.

(The High Window)

Angel's Flight is a funicular railway built at the turn of the century, ostensibly to accommodate the ladies of Bunker Hill who descended with their servants to do their shopping: The line relieved them of the exertion of climbing up the hill on their return. More prosaically, the dirt streets of the day were not suitable for a direct climb up the hill. Billed as the "World's shortest railway," the orange-and-black cable cars took 70 seconds to ascend the 298-foot incline. The two cars were named Olivet and Sinai, after two mountains in the Bible. Closed in the 60's, the railway was reopened in 1996 and ran until February 2001, when one of the cars broke free of the cable and crashed into its sister car. The accident resulted in the death of a tourist and the railway was closed. Not in operation since that time, it is scheduled to reopen in 2003 (the time of this writing). At one time the Third Street Tunnel ran just to the right of the railway; built as a shortcut for streetcars, it has since been closed. In the late 19th century an observation platform above the tunnel provided vistas of the city to those wishing to climb a bit further. Ascend to Bunker Hill via the stairs to the left of the railway.

The first flight has one hundred and twenty-one steps. At the top you will find a small grassy park with benches. Catch your breath here and check out the view. For a better view ascend the next flight of thirty-two steps, which will bring you to the plaza. Continue up the amphitheater steps to the very top of the plaza (Thirty-six steps for a total of one hundred eighty-nine steps). You will now be on same level as the top of the railway. Below and to the east you will see a core of buildings belonging to the Los Angeles of the thirties; behind you and above, to the west, is the Los Angeles of the 21st Century, new, sleek and sterile. Chandler probably would be appalled at the change; or would he see a setting for a story in the darkness of these structures? Perhaps he would surprise us.

View of City Hall from Bunker Hill

Bunker Hill

Bunker is old town, lost town, shabby town, crook town. Once, very long ago, it was the choice residential district of the city, and there are still standing a few of the jigsaw Gothic mansions with wide porches and walls covered with round-end shingles and full corner bay windows with spindle turrets...Out of the apartment houses come women who should be young but have faces like stale beer; men with pulled-down hats and quick eyes that look the street over behind the cupped hand that shields the match flame; worn intellectuals with cigarette coughs and no money in the bank; fly cops with granite faces and unwavering eyes; cokies and coke peddlers; people who look like nothing in particular and know it, and once in a while even men that actually go to work. But they come out early, when the wide cracked sidewalks are empty and still have dew on them.

(The High Window)

Starting in the late 1960s, the area upon which you are standing was designated for urban renewal. The result is the group of buildings in front of you, consisting of a spiral amphitheater, outdoor performance plaza, water court, residential tower and office towers, among other structures. These are designated California Plaza. This stiff, granite-anchored assemblage is the final stage of the redevelopment. To the north, occupied by hotel and office space, is where the Florence Apartments would have been, and where Marlowe finds the body of Mr. George Anson Phillips in the bathroom. None of the Bunker Hill Mansions that are described by Chandler exist today, but you can still see them in movies that were shot on location there. Edward G. Robinson starred in *The Night has a Thousand Eyes* in 1948 and scenes from *The Glenn Miller Story* with Jimmy Stewart were shot here in 1954. The best way to in "see" old Bunker Hill, however, may be through Chandler's eyes his 1938 novella *The King in Yellow*.

This area is now called the "Historic Core". Kiosks provide more information and excellent directions for this area They're well worth stopping to read.

Traffic on Bunker Hill

The Walt Disney Concert Hall under construction.

Los Angeles Public Library, 630 W. Fifth Street

I went over to the Hollywood Public Library and asked questions in the reference room, but couldn't find what I wanted. So I had to go back for my Olds and drive downtown to the Main Library. I found it there...

(The Long Goodbye)

After exploring the plaza, cross Grand Avenue, then walk across the banking plaza to Hope Street. Turn to the left and walk to the Bunker Hill steps. The steps meander down five stories to the Central Library's north entrance. The steps are modern, being built as part of the Bunker Hill Restoration; they are modeled on the Spanish Steps found in Rome and represent an unusual pedestrian experience for auto-oriented Los Angeles. Our route takes you directly through the Library and down to the main (south) entrance on the way to the next stop.

The present Central Library, built in 1924-26, was one of the last buildings designed by Bertrum Goodhue in association with Carleton Monroe Winslow. Goodhue also was architect for the much admired Nebraska State Capitol and his plan for the Library was based upon that structure's design. The library design incorporates Egyptian, Spanish and Byzantine styles with modern geometric elements. The Central Library was located at several other addresses between 1878 and 1926; this building has endured. As you walk down the steps, you will pass the tall circular Gas Company Building on your left. This is also known as the Library Tower. The development of this structure required purchase of the air rights above the Library, necessary to exceed city height restrictions. With the acquired funds, the Library has been able to undertake many renovations. The dominant feature of the building is a tall central tower, topped by a tiled pyramid, which you can see from the steps. Depicted on each side is a mosaic of the sun. At the top of the apex is a hand holding the torch of knowledge (or otherwise; the library has been the site of more than one arson attempt). Running around the building exterior are reliefs by Lee Oskar Lawrie entitled "Meaning and Purpose of Library." These depict various topics that can be researched within the building. Once inside, proceed to the center of the building where the information booth is located. Above you is a multi-colored ceiling mural of recent production. Do not stop your library tour here; there is much more (and better) to come! Take the escalator (to the left) up to the Ledwrick M. Cook rotunda. Overhead in the rotunda are numerous pastel-colored murals depicting the founding of Los Angeles. In the center of the ceiling is a chandelier with a globe and above that a stylized sun, echoing the suns decorating the exterior of the building. The Children's Wing, which was originally the main reading room, is just off the rotunda. Entering this room, observe the many murals and decorative enrichments. The murals, which describe the history of California, were originally located in a tunnel and were moved to this location to preserve and display them more appropriately. The artist, Dean Cornwell, also painted the murals in the Cook rotunda. Overhead are beautifully decorated ceiling beams and panels; these were done by Julian Garnscy, who also did some of the decorative elements in the rotunda. The ornate reading lamps about the room are reproductions of the originals, which were removed in the 1940s.

Retracing your steps, you will find a new extension, called the Thomas Bradley Wing, on the east side of the building. The wing has an enormous atrium running the length of the addition. Green terra cotta tiles decorate a row of giant columns; the innovative chandeliers are worth a look. Four of the stories are above ground and four below. In fact, Lower Level Four is the lowest point in the City of Los Angeles; by coincidence, the top of the Library Tower (Gas Company Building) is the highest point. A Hopi Indian legend mentions that under the site of the library is an underground city, constructed by the lizard people around 3000 BC. This city purportedly runs from the Library to Dodger Stadium, thereby connecting the two bases of civilization: Books and Baseball.

Bookends Café is a pleasant room for coffee or a snack. It features blow-ups of photos from earlier years, among them women in seamed stockings and flapper era hats lined up at a library registration desk. There's also a small patio just off the café.

Returning to the entrance, you may wish to visit the excellent Library Gift Shop. As you leave by the south (Hope Street) entrance, observe the buttress-like piers and terraced entrance on the south (Main) face of the building. These are topped by figurative sculptures; over the entrance are decorative elements and quotations.

Oviatt Building, 617 Olive Street

A MARLOWE MUST-SEE

The Treloar Building was, and is, on Olive Street, near Sixth, on the west side. The sidewalk in front of it had been built of black and white rubber blocks. They were taking them up now to give to the government, and a hatless pale man with a face like a building superintendent was watching the work and looking as if it was breaking his heart.

(The Lady in the Lake)

Exit the library from the south entry, walk down the stairs and go straight to Sixth Street. Take a left on Sixth and walk two blocks to Olive. Take a right at Olive and just around the corner you will find the Oviatt Building, known as the Treloar Building in *The Lady in the Lake*. Take a moment to imagine how those black and white blocks would have looked. In Chandler's book, they are being removed for World War II use, probably as tires.

James Oviatt constructed this steel-framed high-rise building in 1927-28 as a headquarters for his famous Alexander and Oviatt haberdashery. It was designed to have a two-story retail establishment on the main level, with eleven floors of office space above. At the top was a ten-room penthouse, with the exclusive Sadier et Fils Art Deco bar behind a "speak-easy" door. The exterior is described as Italian Romanesque, while the interior is an opulent display of Art Deco. Around the lobby, you will see some of the over 30 tons of glass originally used to decorate the first floor. The glass was designed by Rene Lalique who also designed the metal ornamentation and marble veneer. In the 1970s, portions of the lobby were dismantled and much of the glass and marble removed, however, original pieces remain over the lobby columns and elsewhere. Note the original mallechort-faced elevator doors and other such appointments around the lobby.

A restaurant now takes up the space formerly occupied by the haberdashery. Walking through the lobby and into the restaurant, one transitions from a light and silvery milieu to a dining area done in gilt and dark wood. The vintage light fixtures reflect and direct light up to the golden ceiling, permeating the room with a warm glow. The capitals of each of the wood-paneled columns depict two art nouveau-like female figures facing each other with wings spread behind them. A zigzag frieze runs below the glass-railed second floor balcony. In the middle of the room hangs an extravagant chandelier.

Reproduced with permission.

Ascend the stairs and take a walk around the balcony. You may also take the original (non-self service) elevator, which is still operating. Observe the word *Service* engraved on each of the capitals on the wood columns. Continue and find your way to the bar and lounge. More ambiance awaits you in period-style loungers and chairs situated around the marble dance area. Here you may have a gimlet or martini if you desire. Marlowe couldn't; this was a clothing store when he walked these streets. He would probably have found his way up to the penthouse, however.

The building was much publicized at its opening, due to its extravagant, opulent and avant garde design. James Oviatt lived above the shop. The building was placed on the National Register of Historic Places in 1983.

Reproduced with permission.

Union Station, 800 North Alameda Avenue

A MARLOWE MUST-SEE

There was nothing to it. The Super Chief was on time, as it almost always is, and the subject was as easy to spot as a kangaroo in a dinner jacket...An unhappy girl, if ever I saw one.

(Playback)

Cross Olive Street and find the stop for the north-bound purple DASH bus (B line). The bus will ascend Grand Avenue, pass the west side of the County Courthouse and turn on Temple Street. It will pass the north sides of the Courthouse and City Hall and then turn left onto Los Angeles Street and proceed to Union Station. If you happen to take the orange DASH (D line), you will be deposited at the east end of the Metrolink Depot and have to walk down the tunnel to come out at the Main Station. Prior to the opening of the present terminal in 1939, most train passengers debarked at Pasadena, proceeding to their destinations from there.

The city's desire for a single terminal was fulfilled only after twenty years of wrangling with the three involved railroads before its construction could begin. The depot is one of the gems of the west coast, almost unchanged from the day it was completed and in "mint" condition. Variously described as Mission Moderne, Spanish Colonial

Revival or Spanish Mission, the structure may be best described as "elegant," and a wonderful setting through which actresses such as Bette Davis or Lauren Bacall could stride. The red tile floor of the waiting room is complemented with rows of substantial wood and leather armchairs. A tile frieze in a diamond pattern runs around the inside of the room; massive circular chandeliers hang from the ceiling. Sitting in one of the solid chairs, look up at the ornate ceiling with its dark beams and rust, gold and blue mosaics as well as the other ornate details of the building. Needless to say, the Station has been used in many films, and often was used in Marlowe's time as a photo op for the arrival and departure of movie stars via the *Twentieth Century Limited*. Long distance train departures and arrivals to and from the east are rare, but the Sunset Limited, the Coast Starlight, and the Southwest Chief still serve Los Angeles. The terminal is now primarily used by commuters taking trains to Burbank, Orange County or other nearby environs. A restaurant, Traxx, offers cocktails or dining, should you so choose, but *Tailers* might want to walk across Alameda Street and up two blocks to Philippe the Original, at Ord Street.

Phillipe The Original, 1001 North Alameda

A MARLOWE MIGHT-HAVE-BEEN

This landmark was founded in 1908 by Phillipe Mathieu, an immigrant from France; Phillipe's credo was all you can eat and a pint of claret. The establishment is credited in one variation or another with being the originator of the French Dip Sandwich. In 1927 the business was purchased by Harry, Frank and Dean Martin; the restaurant remains in the family to this day. Although Phillipe has changed location several times since its founding, the present incarnation retains elements of its past. Entering the front door you will find a traditional dark counter, communal tables with individual stools and cement floors with sawdust on them. In the back, the buffet-type line allows customers to select slices from the restaurant's signature roast beef, pork, ham, lamb or turkey, which is then placed on French bread dipped in meat juices. Coleslaw and other condiments are available; the house mustard is hot and the wine is cheap. Check out the row of phone booths and conjecture on whether Marlowe would have made a call from them.

OPTIONAL TOURS

If you parked at one of the Alameda lots, it is now a short stroll of about five blocks to your parking place. From there it is less than a ten-minute drive down Central Avenue to the area where Florian's stood. The La Plata Cigar Factory is a few blocks over from Central. Have a good evening; tomorrow is Marlowe's Hollywood.

Central Avenue

"It was one of the mixed blocks over on Central Avenue, the blocks that are not yet all Negro."

(Farewell, My Lovely)

To drive down Central Avenue, along which Florian's Bar *(Farewell, My Lovely)* was located, retrace your path to Central and drive twenty or thirty blocks in a southerly direction. The Central Avenue area has become more mixed: the blocks close to downtown are primarily Hispanic; further south they change to African-American. Central Avenue is, or was, the cultural and commercial heart of the African-American community in Los Angeles. In Chandler's era, it was known as the Harlem of the West. Starting in the 1950s, the area declined; the nightclubs and rib joints have relocated to other areas of the city or the suburbs. Here and there a run-down bar presents its ragged face to the public, but traces of any nightclubs that look similar to Florian's have disappeared.

LA PLATA CIGAR FACTORY, 2526 GRAND AVENUE

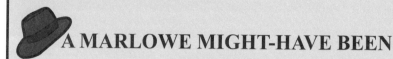

A MARLOWE MIGHT-HAVE BEEN

> *Derek Kingsley marched briskly behind about eight hundred dollars worth of executive desk and planted his backside in a tall leather chair. He reached himself a panatela out of a copper and mahogany box and trimmed it and lit it with a fat copper desk lighter. He took his time about it. It didn't matter about my time. When he had finished this, he leaned back and blew a little smoke...*
>
> *(The Lady in the Lake)*

Philip Marlowe preferred smoking a pipe or cigarettes, but on occasion may have smoked a cigar, as did many of the men he met in his investigations. In his time, many office buildings had their own horseshoe-shaped tobacco counters. These are now gone, but a few minute's drive will bring you to a remaining icon of this era, the **La Plata Cigar Factory.** Return on Central Avenue to Jefferson. Take a left and head west for nine blocks, then go right on Hill, which is one-way, and continue to 26th. Drive around the block and take Grand back down to park in front of the store.

La Plata has been in business for over 50 years and it is likely that Raymond Chandler knew their product; Victor Migenes will be happy to show you the walk-in humidor, containing selected brands of cigars plus the ones they roll right in the building. He has been with La Plata since the age of 16 and became head of the establishment with the retirement of his father, Victor Migenes Sr. in 1983. The La Plata Cigar Company is engaged in production, distribution, wholesale and retail cigar services. Some of their La Plata line is rolled on site while some is imported from Honduras. The lines have been compared to some of the finest imported cigars. Trim one, light it and pretend you are with Derek Kingsley.

One of the authors reflects with Victor Migenes, owner of La Plata.

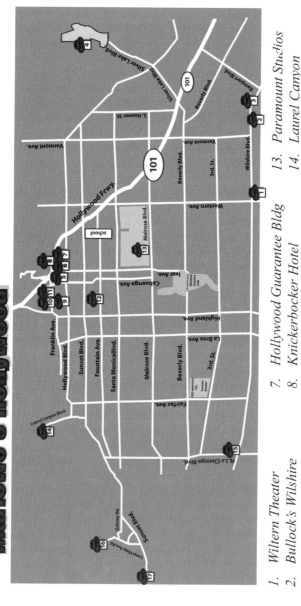

Marlowe's Hollywood

1. Wiltern Theater
2. Bullock's Wilshire
3. Bryson Tower Apartments
4. Silver Lake Reservoir
5. Cahuenga Building
6. Regal Shoes
7. Hollywood Guarantee Bldg
8. Knickerbocker Hotel
9. Musso and Frank Grill
10. Montecito Apartments
11. Chateau des Fleurs
12. Sort of a Bungalow Court
13. Paramount Studios
14. Laurel Canyon
15. Lawry's The Prime Rib
16. Doheny Mansion
17. Beverly Hills Hotel

Marlowe's Hollywood

Second Day Tour

The Hollywood tour begins with three stops in the West Lake neighborhood, just to the west of downtown. Chandler used this locale for scenes in *The Big Sleep* and *The Lady in the Lake*. Following these stops, we move on to Silver Lake, which Chandler referred to as Gray Lake in his work. Chandler lived for a while in the Silver Lake area (always restless, he changed his residence at least once per year) and the house in which he stayed is still there. From Silver Lake, we will continue to the intersection of Hollywood and Cahuenga Boulevards. The intersection has been designated Chandler Square by the City of Los Angeles. Chandler used Hollywood for settings in *The Long Goodbye, The Big Sleep, Little Sister* and *The King in Yellow*. From Chandler Square, it is a short drive via Fountain Avenue to Paramount Studios, where Chandler worked for several years. From there, the tour winds into Laurel Canyon, another area in which Chandler lived, then on to Lawry's, one of Chandler's frequent stops for ribs or steaks, to the Doheny Mansion (Sternwood Mansion in *The Big Sleep)* and finally the Beverly Hills Hotel.

CHANDLER AND HOLLYWOOD

Chandler had a love/hate relationship with Hollywood. In 1941 RKO pictures bought the rights to *Farewell, My Lovely* for $2,000, and in 1942 Twentieth Century Fox purchased *The High Window* for $3,500. This was more than he had received up to that time from all the hard cover runs of these works. In 1943 he was invited to work on the screenplay of James M. Cain's *Double Indemnity* by director Billy Wilder. His office was located at the Paramount Studios campus; according to Chandler, it was the only studio he liked. After years of working alone, he now was able to interact with other writers at a "writer's table" and enjoyed the experience greatly. The script for *Double Indemnity* received an academy award nomination and Wilder gave credit to Chandler, "one of the greatest creative minds."

By 1945, Chandler had tired of Hollywood and in 1946 moved with his wife Cissy to La Jolla. Chandler came to loathe the directors and producers of movies because of the control they wielded over screenwriters. He outlined his dislike, with a few reservations for the producers he worked with, in an article entitled *Writers in Hollywood* for the November, 1945 issue of *The Atlantic Monthly*. *The Little Sister,* not one of Chandler's best-planned novels, is an interesting indictment of Hollywood; several *Tailing* sites are mentioned in the novel. Despite the "tyranny," Chandler found that the money was good, (up to $4,000 per week at Universal) and he put a good deal of it in bonds. By living within their means, he and his wife were able to live comfortably and independently later in life.

Starting Out

First stop of the tour is the Wiltern Theater, located at Western and Wilshire. Those driving from Santa Monica may wish to take the slower and more interesting drive along Wilshire Boulevard rather than the Santa Monica Freeway. The junction of Wilshire with Western will appear just a few minutes after you pass the La Brea Tar Pits. As you motor down Wilshire Avenue, you will be traversing the original Miracle Mile. This parcel of land between La Brea and Fairfax Avenues was designed and developed as a shopping area in the 1920s. The project was constructed with auto traffic in mind, buildings being constructed with wide display windows on their fronts and parking in the rear. Confounding skeptics, the strip became an immediate success, hence the designation "miracle." Although the original "mile" lies roughly between La Brea and Fairfax Avenues, it is considered to extend as far as Bullock's Wilshire, the entire stretch being an example of the American linear downtown.

Los Angeles' First Homicide?

In 1914, ice age human remains were found at La Brea Tarpit Ten. The remains, a skull and partial skeleton, were determined to be those of a woman, 22-24 years of age, four feet ten inches in height and about 9,000 years old. The skull was fractured in a manner consistent with a blow to the head from a blunt instrument. These represent the only human remains ever found at the site; no motive or suspects have been identified. The museum is named for Rancho La Brea, which literally means "tar pits" in Spanish.

The Wiltern looking across Western Avenue

Wiltern Theater, 3790 Wilshire Boulevard (Western Avenue and Wilshire)

A MARLOWE MIGHT-HAVE-BEEN

I went to a late movie after a while. It meant nothing. I hardly
saw what went on. It was just noise and big faces. When I got
home again I set out a very dull Ruy Lopez and that didn't
mean anything either. So I went to bed.

(The Long Goodbye)

Well worth a stop and walk around is the Wiltern Theater. Designed by the firm of Morgan, Walls and Clements, the theater is within a two-story Zigzag Moderne structure called the Pelissier Building (3780 Wilshire Boulevard) above which stands a twelve-story tower with a two-story "penthouse." The site, which had been used as grazing land, was purchased in 1892 by Germain Pellisier. His grandson, Henry de Roulet, constructed the building, which was intended as a showcase for Warner films, in 1931. Chandler undoubtedly passed the building often and perhaps saw some movies there. The building was scheduled to be demolished in 1982 but was saved at the last minute through efforts of the LA Conservancy. This recently restored WPA Art Deco structure retains fabulous elements similar to those at Bullock's Wilshire. The entire building is clad with tile in varying shades of green copper patina. A series of zigzag friezes, metal and tile, run around the lower structure. The zigzag pattern is echoed in panels over the windows; scalloped panels break up the vertically-oriented metal windows on the tower. Take some time to check out the box office in the middle of the lobby. The eight-sided structure is entirely silver-gray with stylized fiddlehead/fern devices on the lower sides and above the glass windows. This is echoed in the frieze around the lobby. Overhead is a radial explosion of fabulous leaf and petal-like designs. Moving over to the building lobby at 3780 Wilshire one walks into a small two-story marble-lined entry. The silvery elevator doors exhibit more zigzags and the light fixtures have intact mallechort diffusers with art deco patterns.

No longer used as a cinema, the Wiltern theater, located a short distance from Bullock's Wilshire, is regularly used for musical and other stage events.

Bullock's Wilshire, 3050 Wilshire Boulevard

A MARLOWE MUST-SEE

"You don't think I'd stooge for Eddie Mars, do you, angel?"
"No-o, I guess not. Not that. I'll meet you in half an
hour. Beside Bullock's Wilshire, the east entrance to the
parking lot."

"Give me the money."
The motor of the gray Plymouth throbbed under her voice and
the rain pounded above it. The violet light at the top Bullock's
green-tinged tower was far above us, serene and withdrawn
from the dark, dripping city. Her black-gloved hand reached
out and I put the bills in it.

(The Big Sleep)

To get to Bullock's, continue east on Wilshire Boulevard from the Wiltern for about a mile. As you approach, you will first see to the right the 241-foot tower, famous for its violet light (now dimmed) and then, under it, the first and arguably the most fabulous suburban department store. The green and tan clad building rests on a base of black marble. The columns guarding the front have green copper panels set between them at their tops. On the columns' capitals are zigzag designs. The tower has an entirely copper "lantern" with braided designs; it is from here that the violet light pierced the night. Facing Wilshire Boulevard are empty display windows; over them are canopies with sunburst patterns on their lower sides. Looking through the windows, you will observe the tables and bookcases of a legal library, for which the building is now used. Built in 1929, the store was intended for customers arriving by automobile; for that reason the main entrance is at the back, adjacent to the parking

lot. On the ceiling of the glass-walled rear portico is an elegant mural in muted green and violet colors depicting the god Mercury, flanked by symbols of early twentieth-century progress:

a zeppelin, an airplane, a luxury liner and a locomotive. A look in at the polished terrazzo floors and mint condition of the structure's appointments indicates the fabulous level of shopping that went on inside. Indeed, the store was a favorite with Greta Garbo, Mae West, Marlene Dietrich, and many others. For more detailed information about this icon of the art deco period, see *Bullocks Wilshire,* by Margaret Leslie Davis, Balcony Press 1996.

Bryson Tower Apartments, 2701 Wilshire Boulevard

...the Bryson Tower, a white stucco palace with fretted lanterns in the forecourt and tall date palms. The entrance was in an L, up marble steps, through a Moorish archway, and over a lobby that was too big and a carpet that was too blue.

(The Lady in the Lake)

Continue down Wilshire for six blocks. The Bryson Tower Apartment building stands on the left on the corner of Wilshire and Rampart Boulevards. *Tailers* should park on Wilshire, as they will be turning left on Rampart to proceed to the next stop. This is one of the rare instances in which, excepting public structures, Chandler uses the actual name of a building. Marlowe indicates that it is on "Sunset Terrace" near Bullock's Wilshire. The white stucco structure has two upraised lions on high pedestals at each side of the front entrance. The name Bryson Towers is engraved under their feet. A locked iron gate prevents entrance except to invited guests. The building has the distinction of having once been owned by Fred McMurray.

The Bryson from across Wilshire Avenue

Silver Lake Reservoir

Gray Lake is an artificial reservoir in a cut between two groups of hills, on the east fringe of San Angelo. Narrow but expensively paved streets wind around the hills, describing elaborate curves along their flanks for the benefit of a few cheap and scattered bungalows.

(Finger Man, *Trouble is my Business*)

Leaving the Bryson, drive up Rampart Boulevard until it intersects Sunset Boulevard. Take a left and drive four blocks to Silver Lake Boulevard. Take a right on Silver Lake Boulevard and proceed about a mile and a half to Silver Lake. Chandler describes stretches without houses in this area, crumbling banks of dirt, gopher holes, wild grass. It is now totally built up, but not with cheap bungalows. During Chandler's time, the lake may have been more accessible. Not a remarkable body of water, it is surrounded with link fence and barbed wire. It is a source of some of Los Angeles' drinking water supply, as it was then. Across the road running by the lake, homes have replaced any cabins that once populated the hills around it. The streets on the hills are still narrow, however, with elaborate curves ascending and descending the slopes. Drive up into them at the risk of becoming lost, if only for a few minutes. Chandler lived for a time to southwest of the reservoir, on Redesdale Avenue.

Chandler Square,
Hollywood and Cahuenga Boulevards

After circumnavigating the reservoir, find Armstrong Boulevard, which intersects with Silver Lake Drive at the north end. About two blocks after the intersection, take a left on Rowena and continue past Hyperion until you reach St. George Street. Take another left. Proceed eight blocks until you reach Franklin Avenue and take a right. Drive about a half mile down Franklin, take a left on Vermont, then drive four blocks to Hollywood Boulevard. Take a right on to the boulevard. Just slightly over a mile and *Tailers* will find themselves at the corner of Hollywood and Cahuenga. Street parking should be available within a block of two of the square.

This intersection was designated "Raymond Chandler Square" on August 5, 1994 by the Los Angeles City Council to recognize the writer who did so much to shape the city's literary landscape. The area is busy, with busses roaring along Hollywood Boulevard and lots of tourists. After you've had a look at the Square and the Cahuenga, you can check out the stars on the sidewalks or do a little shopping. It's a good place to find wigs, watches, tiaras, high heels and flashing earrings, to get a payday advanced or to practice some tae kwan do.

Around Chandler Square are several of the buildings mentioned in Chandler's books, as well as bars and restaurants he frequented, all within walking distance. These include the Cahuenga Building, where Marlowe's office was located, the Montecito Apartments (where Dolores Gonzales lived in *The Little Sister),* Musso and Frank Grill, The Knickerbocker Hotel and The Hollywood Guaranty Building. Various historical plaques are placed throughout the district. On the northeast corner of the square is our first stop and where it all started, the Cahuenga Building.

The Cahuenga Building (above) and a sign on Chandler Square

HOLLYWOOD
HISTORIC
SITE

31

Raymond Chandler Square
Hollywood Blvd at Cahuenga.

*G*angsters, show-girls, filthy rich women, scam artists and a savvy private detective by the name of Phillip Marlowe haunt this intersection. They were the characters in a series of mystery novels written by Raymond Chandler, who designated a fictional building at this intersection - the "Cahuenga Building" - as the central point of Phillip Marlowe's activities. Some believe the bank building on the northeast corner was the inspiration for the "Cahuenga Building", where Marlowe's office was located.

Next Site: 6554 Hollywood Blvd.

TOURING WITH THE HOLLYWOOD DASH

Tailers may wish to take the Hollywood DASH during this segment of the tour. Stops are located along Hollywood Boulevard every two blocks or so. The Hollywood DASH route travels up Vermont to Franklin, west to Highland, then dips down from Franklin to pass through Chandler Square, returning to Vermont via Fountain. The route does not cover all of the locations described here, but is an excellent way to tour the area.

Dash maps for the Hollywood Route are available on the web at http://www.ladottransit.com/dash/index.html or on DASH buses. For more route information, call (213, 310 or 818) 808-2273. *Tailers* may wish to recheck the route map, as it is changed on occasion. Hollywood DASH buses may not be running if it is a weekend or holiday.

The Cahuenga Building from Hollywood Boulevard

Cahuenga Building,
6381-6385 Hollywood Boulevard
(Hollywood and Cahuenga Boulevards)

A MARLOWE MUST-SEE

I drove down to Hollywood Boulevard and put my car in the parking space beside the building and rode up to my floor. I opened the door of the little reception room which I always left unlocked, in case I had a client and the client wanted to wait.

(Farewell, My Lovely)

In Chandler's works, Marlowe's offices were on the sixth or seventh floors of the Cahuenga Building. The building Chandler invented for Marlowe's office was fictional, but probably based on this structure, located at Hollywood and Cahuenga. Unlike his fictional location, the building you see has no seventh floor. The structure was built in 1920-1921, when it was known as the Security Trust and Savings Building. It was designed by John and Donald Parkinson, who also designed Union Station and Memorial Coliseum. In Chandler's time, the Cahuenga was something of a power center of the film industry. Many Hollywood stars kept their accounts and even their jewels in the vaults of Security Trust and Savings (Howard Hughes reportedly kept his baubles there). The style is Italian Renaissance Revival with Romanesque window arches. It has received national recognition and has been designated for historic status. It was renovated in 1985 and again in 1992. Notwithstanding the renovations, it still presents an aura of slight disrepair; it is now used as a "location" for filmmakers.

Regal Shoes,
6349/53 Hollywood Boulevard

 A MARLOWE MIGHT-HAVE-BEEN

Proceed east from the Cahuenga Building on foot. On the way to our destination, the Hollywood Guaranty Building, take a look at the Regal Shoe Building. Did Raymond Chandler purchase his shoes here? He certainly could have. Not mentioned in Chandler's work, the building was constructed in 1939 and is just a few doors down from the Cahuenga. The Streamline Moderne design was by Walker and Eisen, Architects. Vacant at the time this guide was published, the structure has round windows and other elements of ocean liners reminiscent of the Coca-Cola Bottling Building, built in 1934.

The Hollywood Guaranty Building, 6331 Hollywood Boulevard (Hollywood and Ivar)

It was an antique with a cigar counter in the entrance and a manually operated elevator that lurched and hated to level off. The corridor of the sixth floor was narrow and the doors had frosted glass panels. It was older and much dirtier than my own building. It was loaded with doctors, dentists, Christian Science practitioners not doing too good, the kind of lawyers you hope the other fellow has, the kind of doctors and dentists who just scrape along.

(The Long Goodbye)

In *The Long Goodbye,* seeking information from Dr. Vukanich about Roger Ward, Marlowe walks from the Cahuenga Building to the Stockwell Building on Hollywood Boulevard. A building of the same vintage, one which you can enter, is the Hollywood Guaranty Building, originally the Beaux Arts Guaranty Building. One block east of the Cahuenga, it is faced with brick and has a richly detailed lobby entrance. The Guaranty was constructed in 1923 by Austin and Ashley, architects. The Hollywood columnist Hedda Hopper kept her office here. The building, designated an historical structure, is occupied by the Religious

Technology Center and is used as an L. Ron Hubbard Life Exhibition. The staff will be happy to take you on a one-hour tour of the building between 10:30 AM and 4:00 PM, during which you will receive substantial information about Mr. Hubbard's life. For those more interested in Chandler's life, walk north along Ivar Avenue, to the Knickerbocker Hotel.

Knickerbocker Hotel,
1714 Ivar Avenue

*My stomach suddenly felt fine. I was hungry. I went down
to the Mansion House Coffee Shop and ate lunch and got my
car out of the parking lot next to my building.*

(Farewell, My Lovely)

The Knickerbocker was originally built as a luxury apartment house.
The building design is Renaissance Revival/Beaux Arts style, which
was apparently modified with the addition of the facade and marquee
when it was converted into a hotel. It was renowned for the Lido Room
and used for parties by many Hollywood stars. Elvis Presley, Bette
Davis, Cary Grant and others either stayed at the Knickerbocker or
dined at the Lido. Marilyn Monroe was sneaked through the kitchen to
meet her future husband, Joe DiMaggio. Chandler came here for
lunches. The building is reported to be the home of a ghost or two,
including those of D.W. Griffith (who died in the lobby) and Rudolph
Valentino, who was known to do a tango on the Lido dance floor. Faded
and lumpy, the Knickerbocker's rooms are now used as apartments for
the elderly. Entrance to the residential part of the building is restricted,
although a restaurant has been added which is open to the public.

CHANDLER AND BUGSY SIEGAL

A brief review of the tabloids and newspapers of Chandler's era reveals that his books indeed had a basis in fact. Murders, mayhem and mutilations were commonplace in the Los Angeles of the thirties, as was police corruption. The news media's tendency to over-exaggerate these events may have contributed to the negative image of the city and to the ensuing *noir tag* that was placed on fiction and movies of the time. An example of this was the murder of gambling kingpin Les Bruneman in 1937. This was ordered by Bugsy Siegal and although it was common knowledge that Siegal was behind the murder, no attempt was made to bring him to justice. The fact that underworld money was financing city officials in the district attorney's, police and sheriff's offices undoubtedly had much to do with the lack of aggressive investigation.

Steelgrave, the mobster in *The Little Sister*, is probably based on Bugsy Siegal. Like Steelgrave, Siegal came from the east coast and became friends with people in the entertainment industry. He also built a casino in Las Vegas and operated gambling ships outside the three-mile limit. Siegal was later arrested for the murder of Harry Greenberg, a local mobster who was intending to rat on his bosses. During his stay in the county jail, Siegal enjoyed such perks as delivery of meals, use of a telephone and passes to leave the jail, ostensibly for medical care or legal advice, but actually used for dining and entertainment. When reporters from the Los Angeles Examiner followed Siegal to Lindy's Restaurant, where he met for lunch with an actress, the story received front page coverage. This led to the firing of the doctor writing the passes, but not the district attorney nor any other officials of importance. The doctor did reportedly receive over $20,000 from Siegal for his trouble.

Siegal's claim to fame is as the person who built the modern Las Vegas; his fabulous Flamingo hotel and casino was the first of the major hotels that would be built on the Las Vegas strip during the late 1940s and 1950s. Siegal was killed just before midnight on June 20, 1947 at his house on Linden Drive in Beverly Hills, allegedly for skimming millions of syndicate dollars during and after construction of the Flamingo. The 1991 film *Bugsy,* featuring Warren Beatty in the title role, is based upon his life and death.

Raleigh Studios Building, Melrose Avenue, an example of contemporary streamline moderne design

Musso and Frank Grill,
6667 Hollywood Boulevard

A MARLOWE MIGHT-HAVE-BEEN

Return to Hollywood Boulevard and bear west to Musso and Frank's. The Grill is located three or five blocks down Hollywood Boulevard, just after Cherokee Avenue, depending upon whether one takes the north or south side of the street. This establishment may have been a model for Victors, where Marlowe and Terry Lennox had gimlets, or perhaps for Rudy's barbecue. In either case, Chandler is known to have frequented the Grill, along with other Hollywood literati and stars. Included on that list are Joan Crawford, William Faulkner, Nathaniel West, Bing Crosby and Rudolph Valentino. Charlie Chaplain and Humphrey Bogart were regulars.

The Grill was established in 1919 by John Musso and Frank Toulet and is one of the last surviving restaurants of old Hollywood. With a dark wood interior, horse-shoe shaped booths and white table cloths, the business has maintained itself through the years, and is still a stopping place for movie stars and executives. The restaurant is also famous for being a hangout for screenwriters. Included in the list of writers are F. Scott Fitzgerald, Dashiell Hammett, Ernest Hemingway, William Faulkner and, of course, Chandler. A recent use of the restaurant was for a scene in the movie *Oceans 11* where George Clooney and Brad Pitt discuss their plans in one of the red leather booths. The fare is still the basic American-style food that has always been served at Musso and Frank: steaks, shrimp cocktails, corned beef and cabbage. Expect a minimum charge to eat or drink here. Parking is in back of the restaurant for a small charge in the event you wish to dine.

Montecito Apartments, 6650 Franklin Avenue

Chateau des Fleurs, 6626 Franklin

The Chateau Bercy was old but made over. It had the sort of lobby that asks for plush and india-rubber plants, but gets glass brick, cornice lighting, three-cornered glass tables, and a general air of having been redecorated by a parolee from a nut house. Its color scheme was bile green, linseed-poultice brown, sidewalk gray and money-bottom blue. It was as restful as a split lip.

(The Little Sister)

From Musso and Frank walk the two blocks up Cherokee to Franklin Avenue. As you approach the hill that ascends to Franklin, you will see the Montecito Apartments to the left and the Chateau des Fleurs on the right. Either of them could be a candidate for the building in which Dolores Gonzales lived. Entry is restricted to both of these structures. The brass front door of the Montecito has art deco elements at each side. Unlike Chandler's description, the lobby doesn't have glass block or glass tables, but instead standard restrained art deco designs covered in off-white paint. For those wanting to rent, there is a waiting list. Handmade signs for local outings and shopping trips are taped up around the lobby.

Sort of a Bungalow Court,
(Fountain Avenue)

"Will you come over to my place at once? It's Twenty-four-twelve Renfrew---North, there isn't any South---just half a block below Fountain. It's a sort of bungalow court. My house is the last in line, in the back."

Twenty-four-twelve Renfrew was not strictly a bungalow court. It was a staggered row of six bungalows, all facing the same way, but so-arranged that no two of their front entrances overlooked each other... The door was up two steps, with lanterns on each side and an iron-work grill over the peep hole...

(The King in Yellow, *The Simple Art of Murder)*

The tour now proceeds to Paramount Studios. Return to your vehicle and drive west down Hollywood to Highland Avenue, then south five blocks to Fountain. Turn left on Fountain. During the drive of about one mile to Bronson Avenue, observe the small free-standing bungalows as well as the bungalow court apartments mentioned in *The King in Yellow.* Chandler must have been familiar with the street and the buildings on it as well as an observer of the bungalow court phenomenon.

The Bungalow Court Phenomenon

Numbers of bungalow courts were designed and built in urban areas of southern California during the early part of the twentieth century. The first eleven buildings of this style, called bungalows or "court apartments" were constructed in Pasadena in 1909. The concept of community courtyard space possibly was derived from the Mediterranean/Mission courtyard style. Placing numbers of small bungalows facing each other and off-setting their entryways provided semi-private space off the street and allowed mothers to keep an eye on their children while working in the kitchen, which faced the court. The Spanish style was often continued inside of the building, although interiors were built according to the popular "Craftsman" style of the time, with oak woodwork and built-in buffets. This style was later adapted in the design of "motor hotels" that sprang up in the twenties, which often featured bungalows around a common drive.

Bungalow courts served as an economical form of housing for the populace after the end of World War I, when people were moving out of apartments and looking for a house and garden. The style lent itself to this need as well as a lifestyle dependent upon public transportation; bungalow courts tended to be built along streetcar lines. Small in size, bungalows were promoted for their efficiency through built-in, space saving features and amenities such as modern plumbing, electric lights and gas. Many purchasers were young married couples and single women, increasingly employed in office and professional situations.

The bungalow itself is derived from a British design developed in Bengal, India as a solution for comfortable tropical living. In the United States, the bungalow became associated with the Craftsman Movement and the result was a small, clean design that evolved during the early 1900s quite unlike the elaborate Victorian dwellings of previous decades.

Bungalow courts were usually designed to group six to ten houses on two standard city lots, with a central area suitable for a "garden." Interestingly, the style never was used much beyond Southern California. Construction of the courts ceased with most other residential construction during World War II and did not resume after the war. Hundreds of them remain and are preferred by those who want a socially interactive living situation with a garden setting and low maintenance.

Paramount Studios,
5555 Melrose Avenue

The studio cop at the semicircular glassed-in desk put down his telephone and scribbled on a pad. He tore off the sheet and pushed in through the narrow slit not more than three quarters of an inch wide where the glass did not quite meet the top of his desk. His voice coming through the speaking device set into the glass panel had a metallic ring.

(The Little Sister)

At Bronson, turn south and drive two blocks to Santa Monica Boulevard. Turn left, drive one block, turn right and drive for about five or six blocks on Van Ness Avenue towards Melrose Avenue. Find a place to park. We are now on the eastern side of the Paramount Studios property. Walk down to Melrose and proceed west, towards the gates. This is the only studio still located within Hollywood proper. Chandler worked for Paramount on and off during the period 1942 to 1945 and kept an office there. The famous gates through which numerous stars passed are to be found at Bronson Avenue and Marathon Street. Since that time, the studio has added to their property; the gates are now within the studio complex and are not accessible. You may observe them, however, from the entrance at Melrose and Bronson. The DASH bus stops directly in front of them. The main gate to the studio, which echoes the style of the original, is now about a hundred yards further west. Looking across the street to the south, observe the Raleigh Studios Building across Melrose Avenue (see page 69). This is an attractive example of a new Streamline Moderne building done up with modern materials such as tinted glass instead of glass block. Tours of the lots have been suspended since the September 11th, 2001 attacks; we can only hope they will be resumed in the near future.

The famous gates; Chandler passed this way.

Yucca Avenue,
Laurel Canyon

*I was living that year in a house on Yucca Avenue in the
Laurel Canyon district. It was a small hillside house on
a dead end street with a long flight of redwood steps to
the front door and a grove of eucalyptus trees across
the way.*

(The Long Goodbye)

Leaving Paramount, drive west along Melrose and turn right at La Brea
Avenue after about one mile. Continue on La Brea for another mile to
Hollywood Boulevard and turn left. You should now be headed west; at
the end of Hollywood Boulevard, bear right and you will find yourself
on Laurel Canyon Boulevard. Marlowe's house is mentioned as being
in the Laurel Canyon district. It is also just around the bend from
Geiger's place in *The Big Sleep*. A drive of about ten minutes will get
one into the canyon and give a feel for the neighborhood. Enter the
tangle of side roads at your own risk--the roads are rough, hilly and
confusing, and the natives are suspicious.

Lawry's The Prime Rib,
100 North La Cienega Boulevard

*I closed the office and started off in the direction of Victor's
to drink a gimlet, as Terry had asked me to in his letter. I
changed my mind. I wasn't feeling sentimental enough. I
went to Lowry's and had a martini and some prime ribs
and Yorkshire pudding instead.*

(The Long Goodbye)

Hungry? Lawry's The Prime Rib awaits. Returning down Laurel
Canyon Boulevard, continue on Crescent Heights Boulevard until
reaching Beverly Boulevard (about one mile). Take a right and drive
about three quarters of a mile to La Cienega. The building is one half
block north of Wilshire Boulevard on La Cienega.

Lawry's is indeed *the* place where the famous seasoned salt was
invented and is *the* place in Los Angeles for beef lovers. The restaurant
is in a new building, across the street from the location that Chandler
patronized. The modern, low-slung structure echoes the surrounding
contemporary architecture and has a south-facing portico/entry that
vaguely resembles the columns of a Greek temple. Inside, however, the
restaurant still retains its 1930s atmosphere, with uniformed mature
waitresses and table side service. The menu offers four cuts of prime
rib, aged standing rib roasts, something called the Original Spinning
Bowl Salad and of course Yorkshire Pudding. You may wish to have a
martini or a gimlet, either here or at the Beverly Hills Hotel, the last
stop of the day. For more on gimlets and their role in Marlowe's world,
see the sidebar.

REGARDING GIMLETS

gim-let. (OF): N. 1. A small hand tool for boring holes, comprised of a handle with a steel shaft with a pointed cutting end, set perpendicular to the handle. 2. A cocktail made of gin or vodka and sweetened lime juice and sometimes soda.

Although a liquor developed by the Dutch, by the end of the seventeenth century gin had became a distinctly English beverage. English troops sent to the Netherlands in 1585 to fight the Spanish returned to their country with a taste for and apparently the recipes to make this juniper-flavored concoction. A mania for gin overtook England in the early eighteenth century, especially among the common class, and various laws, including the notorious "Gin Act," were passed to curb its consumption. These all failed. Gin's sharp taste probably led to its being mixed with various other ingredients and by the middle of the eighteenth century the gimlet had been invented. According to lore, it was developed by English sailors, "Limeys," who mixed lime juice and sometimes quinine with their gin ration (The quinine mixture became the basis for the gin and tonic). The origin of the name is unknown, although "gimlets," small awl-like tools with corkscrew ends, were certainly used on board ships of that time.

Terry Lennox *(The Long Goodbye)* had a definite opinion about the composition of the gimlet, demanding Rose's Lime Juice in lieu of lime or lemon juice and gin, and mixing the two ingredients in a one-to-one ratio. *Tailing* agrees that Rose's is the best ingredient for a gimlet, but finds the recipe a bit too heavy on the syrup. We prefer them served one-and-a-half or two parts gin to one part Rose's. Make your choice. Most bars serve them with a wedge of lime for those who wish to fine tune the taste. In a wonderfully sexually charged scene in *The Long Goodbye,* Marlowe meets a woman in black (Linda Loring) who drinks gimlets:

The woman in black gave me a quick glance and looked down into her glass. "So few people drink them around here," she said so quietly that I didn't realize at first that she was speaking to me. Then she looked my way again. She had very large dark eyes. She had the reddest fingernails I had ever seen. But she didn't look like a pickup and there was no trace of come-on in her voice. "Gimlets I mean."
"A fellow taught me to like them," I said...The bartender set the drink in front of me. With the lime juice it had a sort of pale greenish yellowish misty look. I tasted it. It was both sweet and sharp at the same time. The woman in black watched me. Then she lifted her own glass towards me. We both drank. Then I knew hers was the same drink..."Perhaps I knew your friend," she said. "What was his name?"..."Lennox," I said. She thanked me for the light and gave me a brief searching glance. Then she nodded. "Yes, I knew him very well. Perhaps a little too well."

(The Long Goodbye)

Doheny Mansion (Greystone), 905 Loma Vista Avenue

 **A MARLOWE MUST-SEE**

The main hallway of the Sternwood place was two stories high. Over the entrance doors, which would have let in a troop of Indian elephants, there was a broad stained-glass panel showing a knight in dark armor rescuing a lady who was tied to a tree...There were French doors at the back of the hall, beyond them a wide sweep of emerald grass to a white garage, in front of which a slim dark young chauffeur in shiny black leggings was dusting a maroon Packard convertible. Beyond the garage were some decorative trees trimmed as carefully as poodle dogs. Beyond them a large greenhouse with a domed roof. Then more trees and beyond everything the solid, uneven, comfortable line of the foothills.

(The Big Sleep)

The beautiful gardens, extravagant and lavish architecture and view of the city make the Doheny mansion and grounds an outstanding stop. It's easy to visualize Marlowe approaching General Sternwood. To get there from Lawry's, head north on La Cienega about a mile, then go left on Sunset Boulevard. After about a mile on Sunset, Doheny Road goes straight, while Sunset veers to the southwest. Stay on Doheny. Turn right at Loma Vista Avenue and follow the signs.

In 1883, Edward Doheny and C.A. Canfield struck oil in Los Angeles. These wells, as well as some discovered in Mexico, made them, for a while, the largest oil producer in the world. The Los Angeles wells were visible from the mansion grounds. "Ned" Doheny, son of Edward and his first wife, Louella Wilkins, was born in 1893. He married Lucy Smith of Pasadena in 1914, and in 1927 construction of the mansion was started on a parcel of land that his father had given to him. Completed in September, 1928, the cost of the building was $1,238,378.00. Designed by Gordon B. Kaufmann, the building is steel-reinforced concrete, faced with Indiana limestone. The walls are three feet thick. Typical of the unique craftsmanship of the building, each of the seven chimneys is of a different style. The craftsmanship continues inside, where railings, banisters and other woodwork were hand carved onsite.

In 1954, 410 acres of the "ranch" were sold and subdivided for a development. The remaining 18.3 acres were purchased by the City of Beverly Hills in 1965 for construction of a water reservoir, which is to the north of the mansion. The grounds were designated a public park. The mansion is not open to the public, but is available to filmmakers, and has been used as a location for movies such as *The Witches of Eastwick, The Winds of War* and *Murder, She Wrote* as well as television series such as *MacGyver*. Once the grounds surrounding the mansion included tennis and badminton courts, horse stables, a swimming pool, a greenhouse and other accouterments. Unfortunately, the greenhouse in which Marlowe has his first encounter with General Sternwood has been removed. Looking through the windows of the mansion, imagine Carmen falling into Marlowe's arms next to the fireplace mantel. The Los Angeles wells that Marlowe speaks of in the book probably describe the ones located on Baldwin Hills. If you look down La Cienaga Avenue and the day is clear, you may be able to see them, still pumping oil.

We can also assume that Baldwin Hills was the setting for Carmen's attempt to kill Marlowe, just as she had earlier killed Rusty Regan. You may wish to drive La Cienaga on your way to or from LAX; it runs right through the Hills.

Beverly Hills Hotel,
9641 Sunset Boulevard, Beverly Hills

A MARLOWE MUST-SEE

A girl in a white sharkskin suit and a luscious figure was climbing the ladder to the high board. I watched the band of white that showed between the tan of her thighs and the suit. I watched it carnally. Then she was out of sight, cut off by the deep overhang of the roof. A moment later I saw her flash down in a one and a half. Spray came high enough to catch the sun and make rainbows that were almost a pretty as the girl.

(The Long Goodbye)

In The Long Goodbye, the address given for the Ritz-Beverly is 1201 Sunset Boulevard. Since then, the street numbers of Hollywood have been made contiguous with those of Los Angeles. The current address of the Beverly Hills Hotel is 9641 Sunset Boulevard. From the Doheny Mansion, drive down Loma Vista and Mountain Drive to Sunset Boulevard. Take a right and proceed a little more than one half mile to where Sunset intersects Beverly Drive. To the right you will see the Beverly Hills Hotel. On the left is a triangle of land, directly in front of the hotel, designated the Will Rogers Memorial Park. Although *Tailing,* unlike Philip Marlowe, does not endorse drinking and driving, taking an hour at the Ritz-Beverly Bar may certainly refresh and enhance one's frame of mind after an afternoon of touring. Non-alcoholic drinks as well as gimlets and martinis are available.

Street parking is usually available outside the grounds, or drive in for valet parking. Walking to the door, you will note impeccably trimmed shrubbery and impeccably trimmed people. At the entrance, ask the concierge or host how to get to the pool bar. He/she will direct you to the right, towards the Polo Lounge. Before you get to the lounge entrance, you will see a flight of stairs going down to your left. Take them past the coffee shop area and follow the signs to the pool. In *The Long Goodbye,* Marlowe drinks scotch and water at the Ritz-Beverly, preferring to have gimlets at Victors; take your pick. The staff will be happy to mix your drink to Terry Lennox's specifications (see his recipe in the *Regarding Gimlets* sidebar). While relaxing, observe the clientele. Alas, there is no longer a diving board, but the pool area, with its pink stucco walls, white trim, mediterranean-blue pool and tables with white umbrellas is delightful. During Chandler's time, it was surrounded by a less elegant cyclone wire fence. Drinks are very good, and the ambiance is priceless. A great place to end your day of touring. If you choose to eat at the Polo Lounge, appropriate dress is required. This ends Marlowe's Hollywood Tour. We will meet in Santa Monica tomorrow for the final tour.

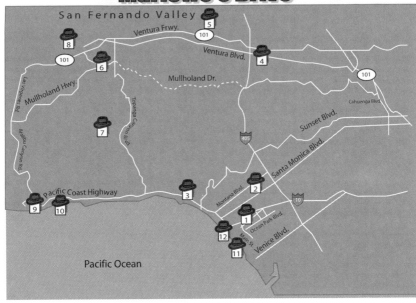

1. *Santa Monica City Hall*
2. *23rd and 25th Streets*
3. *280 Step Stairway*
4. *Mel's Drive-In*
5. *San Fernando Valley*
6. *Mulholland Drive/Highway.*
7. *Santa Ynez Canyon*
8. *Verringer's Ranch*
9. *Malibu Beach Colony*
10. *Malibu Pier*
11. *Santa Monica/Venice Beach Walk*
12. *Santa Monica Pier*

Third Day Tour

Bay City in Chandler's work is based on the City of Santa Monica, with elements of Venice and perhaps Marina Del Rey thrown in. *The High Window, Farewell, My Lovely,* and *The Long Goodbye* all take place in or around these ocean front communities. This tour explores Marlowe's sleuthing in Bay City, then ventures inland to follow the drive he took in *The Little Sister,* loops through the San Fernando Valley and returns to Santa Monica via Malibu. The tour ends at the Santa Monica pier.

Santa Monica City Hall,
1685 Main Street

*It was a cheap looking building for so prosperous a town. It
looked like something from out of the Bible belt. Bums sat
unmolested in a long row on the retaining wall that kept the
front lawn-now mostly Bermuda grass-from falling into the
street. The building was of three stories and had an old belfry
at the top, and the bell still hanging in the belfry. They had
probably rung it for the volunteer fire brigade back in the old
chaw-and-spit days.*

(Farewell, My Lovely)

Start the day by finding Main Street in Santa Monica. City Hall is located on Main between Pico Boulevard and Colorado Avenue and has a parking lot in front. The present-day City Hall is a white structure built in 1938 in what is described as Classic/Moderne style (apparently adding the final "e" to Modern lent credibility to the architectural style). The style emerged during the 1930s as the more exuberant and expensive Art Deco style of the 1920s was passing. Buildings constructed in this style were long, low and streamlined and usually of commercial use.

The building was commissioned under the Federal Emergency Administration and is an example of the many public works projects sponsored by the federal government in the 1930s. Architects were Donald B. Parkinson and J.M. Estep, who also designed Bullock's Wilshire Department Store. Compare this to the Coca-Cola factory, which is an extreme example of "Streamliner Moderne" style. The present structure is most likely not the one that Chandler describes in *Farewell, My Lovely*. The novel was published in 1940, was written during construction of the new building and probably was conceived before construction commenced. What Chandler described appears to be the previous City Hall, which was built in 1902 and dedicated March 19, 1903. The building is no longer standing. In comparison to the old Spanish mission-style building with its three story tower and belfry, the 1938 structure is squat, smooth and wide, with a low, ziggurat-like central tower and no sign of a belfry. Entering the doors, you will see brown and terra cotta colored tiles on the floor of the lobby, with the Santa Monica City Seal in the center. Blue, yellow and terra cotta tiles were used for the wainscot that runs along the walls and anodized aluminum railings may be seen on the second floor balcony. Two murals flank the door, describing the history of Santa Monica from 1769 to 1939, when the city hall was completed. The building was designated a Santa Monica Landmark in 1979. An occasional unmolested bum may still be observed resting on the municipal property.

For a glimpse of where the old city hall stood, drive down Main to Colorado (towards the downtown), take a right on Colorado, then left on Fifth to Santa Monica Boulevard and find parking. Here on the northwest corner of the intersection of Fifth and Santa Monica, in front of a Citibank, is a plaque designating its former location (Santa Monica Boulevard was formerly named Oregon Avenue).

Santa Monica City Hall, circa 1906. Reproduced with permission of the Santa Monica Public Library Image Archives

Fifth Street and Santa Monica Boulevard; site of Marlowe's City Hall.

SANTA MONICA AND THE GAMBLING SHIPS

Santa Monica had a reputation for corruption during the early part of the twentieth century, although the situation was probably geographically inevitable due to its convenient beach front and access to bootleg liquor from Mexico (Prohibition was in effect from 1920 until 1935). Other vices were available from the Santa Monica beach: In the 20s and 30s gambling ships moored just beyond the three mile limit of state and federal jurisdiction. Water taxis ferried patrons from the numerous piers out to the boats. One of the most famous of the gambling ships was the Rex, moored in Santa Monica Bay and owned by ex-rumrunner Tony Cornero Stralla. The Rex catered to the middle class and was unusually successful, operating 24 hours a day with up to 3,000 people on board at any one time. This is possibly the model Chandler chose for the *Montecito* and its owner, Brunette. Under pressure from the State Attorney General, Earl Warren (later justice of the US Supreme Court), the ships finally were closed in 1938-39. Recommissioned, the Rex was sunk off the coast of Africa during World War II.

Santa Monica Pier, described on page 109

23rd and 25th Streets, Santa Monica

...The house was on a corner. It was a cool moist night, no moon...The sign on the corner said Descanso Street. Houses were lighted down the block. I listened for sirens. None came. The other sign said Twenty-third Street. I plowed over to Twenty-fifth Street and started towards the eight-hundred block. No. 819 was Anne Riordans's number. Sanctuary.

(Farewell, My Lovely)

From the old City Hall site, keep going down Fifth to Wilshire Boulevard where you can turn right and drive to 23rd Street. Go left on 23rd. This street is the area of the "hospital" in which Marlowe is kept and drugged in *Farewell, My Lovely*. Most of the structures are single family dwellings, but at Montana Avenue there is a commercial-appearing building that might have been the model for Marlowe's hospital prison. Turn right on Montana and go to 25th Street. The houses in this neighborhood were here when Chandler wrote his novels, and are certainly what he had in mind when he described the above scene. Ann Riordan's house was allegedly located at 819 25th Street, but there is no such number.

The 280-Step Stairway
17572 Pacific Coast Highway at Castellammare

 A MARLOWE MUST-SEE

*Above the beach the highway ran under a wide concrete arch
which was in fact a pedestrian bridge. From the inner end of
this a flight of concrete steps with a thick galvanized handrail
on one side ran straight as a ruler up the side of the mountain...I
walked back through the arch and started up the steps. It was
a nice walk if you liked grunting. There were two hundred and
eighty steps up to Cabrillo Street. They were drifted over with
windblown sand and the handrail was as cold and wet as a
toad's belly.*

(Farewell, My Lovely)

There is no single stairway with two hundred and eighty steps along the
coast highway. Nevertheless, a series of stairways exists and they are
accessible from the beach.

Enter the Pacific Coast Highway (PCH) via California Avenue. Ignore
the first pedestrian bridge. After about three minutes, you will pass
Gladstone's, another local landmark, on the left. Just after Gladstone's
note an overhead pedestrian bridge: This is the entry point to the stairs.
Since traffic is fast on this stretch of highway, by now you will
undoubtedly have overshot your destination. Don't panic! The
continuation of the tour requires us to reverse our course. Continue to
the next light, turn around and retrace the route back to the bridge.
Parking should be available along the beach side of the Pacific Coast
Highway just before the bridge. Watch out for the tow away zones.
Beach parking is also available immediately to the right of the bridge as
one passes back under it. If the surf is up or if it is a weekend, parking
spots may be scarce.

Chandler called this community Montemar Vista. The pedestrian
bridge, officially at 17572 Pacific Coast Highway, can be accessed
from either side of the highway. Since we should be on the beach side,
take the stair up and cross over the highway. *Tailing* is not counting the
bridge steps, although you may desire to do so.

The first section of Marlowe's stairs ascends in three flights, a total of forty steps. Notice security signs popping up like daisies amongst the houses and designating armed response to intruders. This would not have fazed Marlowe; we are more cautious and stay on the stairs. Cross Castellammare Drive and continue up the next section, three flights and a total of sixty-nine steps. Perhaps starting to breath harder, we emerge on Posetano Road and see another stairway. Continue. This section is made up of four flights and a total of one hundred and eighteen steps. Along the way note board fences on one side of the stairs and agave plants and "blue chalk stick" ground cover blanketing the slopes on the other side.

Emerging at the top, we look across Revello Drive and see the remnants of the last flight of steps, which has collapsed. Steps so far: two hundred and twenty-seven, fifty-three steps short of Marlowe's climb. Turn and check the view of the ocean and coastline - on a sunny day it is priceless, and well worth the climb! For more punishment, bear to the left down Revello Drive, which dead ends at this spot for the same reason the stairs end: mud slides. About one hundred yards down the road, at the junction of Revello Drive and Posetano Road, is another section of stairs: three flights and eighty-six steps. This gets us past Marlowe's two hundred and eighty! These are poorly maintained and like the others end with a whimper at the top; ascend and descend with caution!

In *Farewell,* when Marlowe gets to the top of the stairs, he walks to 4212 Cabrillo Street, where Lindsay Marriott lives. Marriott asks Marlowe to walk up from the sidewalk café along the highway, since the way up to the house is twisting and confusing by automobile. The basis for the café appears to be gone, and also that for Marriott's dwelling.

Lavery's House, Dr. Almore and the death of Thelma Todd

In *The Lady in the Lake*, Marlowe drives to Altair Street, which is at the end of a deep canyon, to investigate Chris Lavery. Driving to the site of the 280 Steps, we have passed Pacific Palisades, the area Chandler probably had in mind when he described Lavery's house. In the book, Dr. Almore's wife has committed suicide several years previous, although there is some suspicion about the manner of her death, which was by carbon monoxide poisoning. The inspiration for this may have come from the demise of actress Thelma Todd in 1935. Todd was found dead one December morning sitting in her car in the garage of her house. The cause of death was ruled to be asphyxiation, either accidentally or by suicide. It was speculated that she may have been murdered, either by mobsters or by a former lover or husband. In any case, the mystery was never solved, and the events leading to her death remain unknown.

Overpass leading to stairway at Castellammare

Marlowe's Drive

There was nothing lonely about the trip. There never is on that road. Fast boys in stripped-down Fords shot in and out of the traffic streams, missing fenders by a sixteenth of an inch, but somehow always missing them. Tired men in dusty coupes and sedans winced and tightened their grip on the wheel and ploughed on north and west towards home and dinner.

(The Little Sister)

The drive upon which we are embarking takes in elements of Marlowe's route as described in Chapter Thirteen of *The Little Sister.* Marlowe is in a dark mood as he starts the journey, reflecting on the murder he has discovered and wondering what his business really is about. Along the way, he eats a quick and unsatisfying meal at a chain restaurant, tosses off a brandy at a bar, and continues on to Oxnard. Our route will turn off long before Oxnard, cross to Mulholland Drive and down to Malibu before returning to Santa Monica.

Descending the steps, head back into Santa Monica and drive to Hollywood via the Santa Monica Boulevard. Here we take a left on Highland Avenue and drive through the heart of Hollywood to West Cahuenga Boulevard. Passing the glitz of downtown Hollywood, we go by the Hollywood Bowl. At this point, stay to the left and go onto West Cahuenga (If you go straight, you will find yourself on the Hollywood Freeway. Should this happen, take the next exit to get back on to West Cahuenga). On the left, we pass the east entrance to Mulholland Drive, which meanders along the Santa Monica Range overlooking Los Angeles, and with which we will reconnect at the end of the drive. After about two and a half miles, we pass over the crest of a hill and see Universal City. At this point, Cahuenga Avenue becomes Ventura Boulevard.

What appears before us is similar to what Marlowe described, but updated and revised with the passage of time. To the left is the valley side of the Santa Monica Mountains, in front of which are motels, shopping malls, burgers, discount clothing, casting agencies, night clubs, hair studios, auto repair, sushi, glass office buildings, palm trees and elderly folks with goggle sunglasses. As we continue, the Boulevard changes, becomes older and in some stretches has remnants of vintage stucco one- and two-story commercial buildings.

Mel's—A fixture on Ventura Boulevard

Mel's Drive-In,
14846 Ventura Boulevard, Sherman Oaks

 A MARLOWE MIGHT-HAVE-BEEN

...I drove on past the gaudy neons and the false fronts behind them, the sleazy hamburger joints that look like palaces under the colors, the circular drive-ins as gay as circuses with the chipper hard-eyed carhops...

(The Little Sister)

After about eight miles on Ventura Boulevard, Studio City will have imperceptibly turned into Sherman Oaks. Take a left on Kester and park in the lot behind Mel's. Mel's has the distinction of being one of the first drive-in chains in California. A Mel's Drive-In (not this one) was featured in the movie *American Graffiti*. This particular location has been in existence since the 1930s and was originally a diner, not a drive-in, being purchased by the chain at a later date. The building has maintained its authentic appearance, from the Rock-Ola jukebox at the door to the metal-trimmed counters and tables and green and white trimmed booths. Juke box selections may be made from each booth and kid's meals are available in boxes in the shape of vintage 50s automobiles.

The food is good and the wait staff is perky and efficient. It's easy to imagine Marlowe eating a meal at a previous incarnation of Mel's. You can still order a chicken pot pie, a blue-plate special, or great burgers, malts, and everything that goes with American drive-ins of this vintage. In the 30s, Marlowe would have been greeted by a server wearing a uniform: slacks, jacket with an ascot, and a military-style campaign hat. Would he have eaten here? Maybe. Certainly Chandler passed here on his drives and perhaps stopped for coffee (adding a jolt from his flask).

San Fernando Valley

*The wind was quiet out here and the valley moonlight was so
sharp that the black shadows looked as if they had been cut
with an engraving tool.*

*Around the curve the whole valley spread out before me. A
thousand white houses built up and down the hills, ten thousand
lighted windows and the stars hanging down over them politely,
not getting too close...*

(The High Window)

Although the municipalities along this fifteen-mile drive change
frequently, strip commercial is a constant. Whether at the start or the
end, one observes more sushi and burgers, casting agencies and motels,
banks and dollar stores, and acres and acres of free parking. It's not
hard to pick up a feel for the area as Marlowe would have, even after all
these years.

Ventura Boulevard continues through Sherman Oaks, Encino, Tarzana,
and into Woodland Hills. Although now typical in many United States
cities, what you are driving is one of the original strips. Chandler must
have despised it, yet may have found its vitality seductive. To the right
we pass the San Fernando Valley and tracts of houses, once and perhaps
still occupied by the tired men Marlowe describes, waiting for their
dinners.

In *The High Window,* Marlowe drives through the San Fernando Valley
on the way to Idle Valley, a gated community in the foothills. Looking
back from the club, he sees the valley laid out before him in the night.
Some of these small and exclusive enclaves are still found in the valley
and might have been the basis for his description.

After Tarzana, be on the lookout for Topanga Canyon Boulevard in
Woodland Hills. Take a left and drive up to Mulholland Drive and go
right on the Drive. Within a mile the road splits into Mulholland
Highway and Mulholland Drive. Stay to the left, on the Highway (The
Drive goes back north, into the valley). After about on quarter of a
mile, pull over to the right and look back to see a vista of the valley. If
it has recently rained, you might notice the smell of pines and the
tomcat smell of eucalyptus trees.

Mulholland Highway

*Then the paved avenue ended abruptly in a dirt road packed as
hard as concrete in dry weather. The dirt road narrowed and
dropped slowly downhill between walls of brush. The lights of
the Belvedere Beach Club hung in the air to the right and far
ahead there was a gleam of moving water. The acrid smell of
the sage filled the night.*

(Farewell, My Lovely)

We are now in Calabasas. A mile further on the Mulholland Highway and
you will be in a relatively undeveloped area. To the right is a high school,
tennis courts and the accouterments of suburban living; to the left are hills
and pasturage for herefords and horses. These buildings soon give way to
long-needled pines, pinion, spruce, manzanita and sage. The area is lush and
prone to mud slides during the winter rains and dry and flammable in the
summer. Depending upon the season and the circumstance, parts of the
highway may be closed. The area of Mulholland Drive lying behind us,
between Sepulveda and Topanga Canyon Boulevards, has been closed for
these reasons and is accessible only by foot, mountain bike or four wheel
drive vehicle.

Named after William Mulholland, the self-educated Irish engineer who
brought water to Los Angeles, Mulholland Drive and Highway meander for
50 miles along the ridge of the Santa Monica Mountains from Cahuenga
Pass to Leo Carillo State Park. The peaks of the Santa Monica Mountains
have been used as the backdrop for numerous television shows and movies.
They were used as a backdrop for the series *Mash,* which was set in the
mountains of Korea. You'll find amazing views of spectacular houses,
spectacular cliffs, and park lands - which is what Marlowe must have seen
during his drive. Today the area is home to stars and the wealthy.
According to various tour companies, Marlon Brando, Annette Benning and
Warren Beatty live or maintain houses along the route.

Past the development, the drive becomes more rural. Stop for a few minutes
and you will be amazed at how quiet the area is compared to the clatter of
the city just a few minutes before. The call of a crow and the wind in the
pines may be the only sounds that break the silence. Native wildlife is still
found in the mountains: golden eagles, coyote, mountain lions and deer.
One is hardly aware of being a few minutes from one of the largest
metropolitan areas in the United States.

WILLIAM MULHOLLAND

Born in Belfast, Ireland, William Mulholland left home at the age of 15, which also marked the end of his formal education. Following stints at sea as an apprentice, work in lumber camps and for his uncle in Pittsburgh, he arrived in San Francisco in 1877. The same year he moved to the Los Angeles area after a brief job mining in Arizona.

One of his first jobs in Los Angeles was maintenance of the water ditches which carried water to reservoirs. His spare time was spent studying books on hydraulics, mathematics, geology and other subjects relevant to his future work. Silver Lake Reservoir, described in *Marlowe's Hollywood,* is an early (1906) example of his work. His life's work, however was construction of the aqueduct from the Eastern Sierras to Los Angeles. Along with his former boss, Fred Eaton, Mulholland focused on the Owens River, 200 miles to the east, as a plentiful source of water for the growing city. Through land purchases, political means and deceit, the two had managed by 1905 to acquire much of the Owens Valley land and water rights, to the anger of its residents. A multi-million dollar bond issue by the City of Los Angeles in 1905 made the project a reality.

Construction of the aqueduct employed thousands of men and took eight years; it was considered one of the greatest engineering efforts of the time. The first water flowed from this source on November 5, 1913. Interestingly enough, the city had no use for most of the water and much of it was diverted to the San Fernando valley, to land that Eaton's friends had purchased prior to the construction of the aqueduct. Owens valley agriculture was now in ruins and the rage of its landowners led to several successful sabotage efforts against the pipeline. Despite these efforts, the Owens Valley resistance had faded by 1927. The movie *Chinatown* uses many elements of the politics behind the building of the aqueduct in its story line, placing it at a later date than the actual events.

Prior to construction of the aqueduct, Los Angeles' population was about 320,000 and would have been limited to 500,000 with existing water resources. By the end of the 1920s it had grown to over one million. A grateful populace rewarded Mulholland by naming the scenic drive along the crest of the Santa Monica mountains after him shortly after completion of the aqueduct.

At the peak of his career, Mulholland was acclaimed as one of the greatest engineers of the age and was much sought after as a consultant and speaker. This was brought to an end in 1928 by the failure of one of his other engineering marvels, the St. Francis Dam. The dam was located in San Francisquito Canyon, near present-day Santa Clarita. Completed in 1926, the 200-foot structure was designed to be a regulating reservoir and power-generating dam, as well as a source of water in the event of a cut-off of water from Owens Valley.

On the morning of March 12, 1928, the damkeeper reported a leak near the western abutment of the dam. Mulholland made an inspection that same day and declared the leaks normal for this type of dam. At 11:57 that night, the dam burst, releasing a wall of water that would wreak havoc along the 58-mile course of the Santa Clara River to the Pacific Ocean. The flood cost over $7,000,000 in property damage and 500 lives were lost. It was later determined that geological abnormalities as well as hydraulic pressures unknown to the engineers of the time had contributed to the dam's failure. The disaster effectively ended Mulholland's career. Grief-stricken and haunted by the disaster, he ended his life a semi-recluse. The triumph and tragedy of William Mulholland represent a fascinating chapter in the history of Los Angeles. This remarkable man may truly be credited with having made possible the present metropolis.

Silver Lake Dam--a Mulholland project

Santa Ynez Canyon

Then a white-painted barrier loomed across the dirt road...I switched the lights off altogether and got out of the car. The crickets stopped chirping. For a little while the silence was so complete that I could hear the sound of tires on the highway at the bottom of the cliffs, a mile away. Then one by one the crickets started up again until the night was full of them.

(Farewell, My Lovely)

Below the stretch of highway upon which we are driving, several canyons branch off along the coast highway and wind their way up the foothills. One of these Marlowe called Purissima Canyon. It is there that Marlowe drove with Lindsay Marriott to deliver $8,000, and where he left the car only to be sapped down, regaining consciousness to find his employer dead. There is an actual Santa Ynez Canyon; however, it is a long and difficult climb that ascends from near Palisades Drive. The trailhead is at the end of Verenda de la Montura and is not for the casual stroller. The trail climbs almost to the Mulholland Highway, but does not connect, ending about 1 ° miles below it.

Verringer's Ranch, Sepulveda Canyon

Back from the highway at the bottom of Sepulveda Canyon were two square yellow gateposts. A five-barred gate hung open from one of them. Over the entrance was a sign hung on wire: PRIVATE ROAD. NO ADMITTANCE. *The air was warm and quiet and full of the tomcat smell of eucalyptus trees.*

(The Long Goodbye)

Somewhere to the north of this drive was the ranch in *The Long Goodbye,* twenty miles up from West LA. Parts of Mulholland Highway have been slowly turned into a development of modern semi-estates and gypsum board castles, but as we drive further west, it gives way to country that is rugged and still occupied by working ranches. Some of the route remains very much as it was when Marlowe made his drive.

When you get to Las Virgenes Road take a left. Las Virgenes branches at Malibu Canyon Road after about one half mile. Go straight on Malibu Canyon Road. Descending on the road, we pass the bright white structures of the Aswin Hindu Temple to the left. This part of the tour winds through rugged, steep canyons of boulders and mud, waiting to wash down during the next torrent. After a few miles, the narrow and winding road opens to a view of the Pacific Ocean. If it is dusk, the lights of Santa Monica will be visible in the distance, slowly winking on.

Malibu Beach Colony/
Bel Air Bay Club Castellammare

Malibu. More movie stars. More pink and blue bathtubs. More tufted beds. More Chanel No. 5. More Lincoln Continentals and Cadillacs. More wind-blown hair and sunglasses and attitudes and pseudo-refined voices and waterfront morals. Now, wait a minute. Lots of nice people work in pictures. You've got the wrong attitude, Marlowe. You're not human tonight.

(The Little Sister)

Coming down on Malibu Canyon Road, we meet the Pacific Coast Highway (PCH). Take a right on the PCH and then a left at Webb Way, about a half mile. The Malibu Colony shopping area is located here. Although not here when Marlowe drove by, it is a good place to take a break and have a cup of coffee or refreshment. Continue left at the frontage road, driving slowly and you will pass the gated entrance to the Malibu Colony before merging back on to the Pacific Coast Highway.

Chandler referred to the Colony as the Del Rey beach club and located it in Castellammare. The Colony was used as the location of Roger Wade's house in the 1973 Robert Altman film adaptation of *The Long Goodbye*. The only way to get any closer to the Colony is from Malibu Lagoon State Beach, our next stop.

Malibu Pier/Malibu Lagoon State Beach

*I smelled Los Angeles before I got to it. It smelled stale and old
like a living room that had been closed too long. But the colored
lights fooled you. The lights were wonderful. There ought to be
a monument to the man who invented neon lights. Fifteen stories
high, solid marble. There's a boy who really made something out
of nothing.*

(The Little Sister)

For a view of Malibu Pier or a closer look at the Malibu Beach Colony, take
a right at the first signal light after the Colony, about one-quarter mile. This
leads to Malibu Lagoon State Beach. One can observe all manner of
aquatic birds in the park and whales can often be seen from the shore. The
information kiosks describe how this whole area is creeping to the
northwest at a rate of two inches per year. The park contains a salt estuary
and protected wetlands and there is an enjoyable nature walk and hike to the
surf. The Chumash Indians noted the characteristic of this area, calling it
"Humaliwo" meaning "when the surf sounds loudly."

The 780-foot pier with its famous restaurant (Alice's) at the land end is
closed due to storm damage. The sea end of the pier formerly held a bait
shop. It was constructed at the turn of the twentieth century by the
Frederick Rindge family for mooring yachts. The area just west of the pier
is Surfrider's Beach and when the waves are up or the wind is right, the lot
will be filled with vehicles of surfers. This area is also famous for being the
location of many of the 50s beach party movies and has also been used as a
location for *Baywatch* and *The Rockford Files.*

As one strolls to
the water, the
homes of the
colony will be on
the right. If you
desire to walk the
beach in front of
homes belonging
to celebrities,
you may do so. Despite the privacy signs, the beach is public right-of-way
as long as one stays below the high tide mark. Walking the other way, you
will be able to see the Malibu Pier and the Coastline curving away past the
pier to Santa Monica.

Santa Monica/Venice Beach Walk

A MARLOWE MUST-SEE

I lay on my back on a bed in a waterfront hotel and waited for it to get dark. It was a small front room with a hard bed and a mattress slightly thicker than the cotton blanket that covered it...The reflection of a red neon light glared on the ceiling. When it made the whole room red it would be dark enough to go out. Outside cars honked along the alley they call the Speedway. Feet slithered on the sidewalks below my window. There was a murmur and mutter of coming and going in the air.

(Farewell, My Lovely)

Returning along the Pacific Highway, drive through Santa Monica and into Venice. To get a feeling for what existed during Philip Marlowe's time, walk back from the beach a block or two to one of the narrow streets between Pacific Avenue and Main in Venice. Keep an eye out for the alley called Speedway, one-half block up from Ocean Front. The cross streets have names like Ozone, Dudley, Thornton and Breeze. Along them can be found bungalows and Spanish villas of the type Marlowe would have visited. Still standing in Venice, they are disappearing in Santa Monica, replaced by townhouses and mini-mansions. Walking northwest along the Venice/Santa Monica beachwalk one passes the sun glass shops, bars, hot dog stands and assorted detritus of the Venice milieu. All this chaos ends abruptly at the Santa Monica City Line, after which a park-like setting prevails. Continue along the beach; in the distance the Santa Monica pier juts into the dark sea. A twenty-minute walk, and we hear the calliope and smell the unique aromas of the pier.

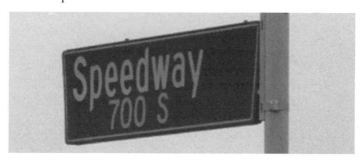

Santa Monica Pier

A MARLOWE MUST-SEE

*Then I sought out a restaurant that didn't smell of frying grease
and found one with a purple neon sign and a cocktail bar behind
a reed curtain. A male cutie with henna'd hair drooped at a
bungalow grand piano and tickled the keys lasciviously and
sang* Stairway to the Stars *in a voice with half the steps missing.*
(Farewell, My Lovely)

At one time there were many entertainment piers along the beach from
Pacific Palisades to Long Beach The present Santa Monica pier is
actually two piers that have been joined together. The first of these, the
1600-foot Santa Monica Municipal Pier, was completed in 1909. A
companion 1080-foot pier, built by Charles Looff in 1916, featured the
Hippodrome building (which now houses a carousel) a roller coaster and
assorted thrill rides. Storms and changing tastes took their toll, and by
the 70s, the pier was earmarked to be dismantled. The subsequent
outcry resulted in the Pier being established as a Los Angeles County
Historical Landmark. In the 80s, the Pier was extensively reinforced
and restored; it now welcomes over three million visitors per year.

Standing on the walk, one can imagine Marlowe going down to the
ocean under the pier where the water taxis docked and bumping into a
redheaded roughneck coincidentally named Red, an ex-policeman with a
boat. After striking a deal, he walks slowly down the line to another
pier, black and brooding without lights, where he meets Red again, goes
down the seasteps and in ten minutes is underway to the waiting
Montecito and his meeting with the casino owner, Brunette.

And here, dear *Tailer*, we end our tour, looking out over the dark
Pacific, amid reflecting lights, crashing surf and the sounds and smells
of the pier. We have touched another time, gathered what we could of
what remains and can only dream of the rest. It is our hope that you
have enjoyed your journey as much as we enjoyed compiling this guide.

Acknowledgments

A special thanks to the following people, whose assistance was invaluable to the project:

- Laurie Schlueter-Hynes, who did the page design.
- Meleck Davis, whose graphic design provided a theme and continuity to the text.
- Our proof readers: Randall Olson, Joyce Bigiani and Peter Nord.
- Management of the Bradbury and Oviatt Buildings for interior photo permission.
- Staff of the Santa Monica and Los Angeles libraries, who assisted in our research.
- Gerry Schlueter, for technical advice.

Website

Anyone having comments or questions about this guide or desiring to order more copies, please visit our website:

burlwrite.com

Books by Raymond Chandler

The Big Sleep, 1939
Farewell, My Lovely, 1940
The High Window, 1942
The Lady in the Lake, 1943
The Little Sister, 1949
The Long Goodbye, 1953
Playback, 1958

Short Story Collections by Raymond Chandler

The Simple Art of Murder, 1950
Trouble is My Business, 1950

Bibliography

Davis, Margaret Leslie, *Bullocks Wilshire*. Los Angeles: Balcony Press 1996.

Frommers. *Los Angeles*. New York, New York: Hungry Minds, Inc., 2001.

Insight Guides. *Los Angeles*. Third Edition. Maspeth, New York: Langenscheidt Publishers, Inc., 2000.

Los Angeles Conservancy Archives

Marling, William. *Raymond Chandler*. Boston: Twayne Publishers, 1986.

MacShane, Frank. *The Life of Raymond Chandler*. New York: E. P. Dutton, 1976.

Skinner, Robert. *The hard-boiled explicator: a guide to the study of Dashiell Hammett, Raymond Chandler, and Ross Macdonald*. Metuchen, NJ: Scarecrow Press, 1985.

Weil, Martin Eli, *Text Prepared for nomination of the building to the National Register of Historic Places*. Ratkovich, Bowers Incorporated. October, 1982.

Ward, Elizabeth and Silver. Alain. *Raymond Chandler's Los Angeles*. Woodstock, New York: The Overlook Press, 1987.

Wolfe, Peter. *Something More Than Night: The Case of Raymond Chandler*. Bowling Green, Ohio: Bowling Green State University Popular Press, 1985.

View of the Pacific from Marlowe's Drive